IRISH AISLES ARE SMILING

Annabelle Archer Wedding Planner Mystery #13

LAURA DURHAM

Broadmoor Books

For Claire and Rose
I didn't make either of you the victim or the killer, but I hope this is just as fun!

I

"Stay to your left," I screamed as a stone wall grazed the passenger side mirror, and I instinctively leaned toward Richard.

"I'm on the left, Annabelle," he said, his knuckles white and his face glued to the road in front of us, what little of it there was. His dark hair--usually perfectly styled with plenty of product--looked disheveled, and his artificially tanned skin was a shade or two paler than usual.

Kate leaned her head between the two front seats, flicking a strand of blond hair out of her eyes. "Are you sure we're not on a one-way street? This doesn't look wide enough for two cars."

"Positive," I said, one hand holding up the road map of Ireland they'd given us at the rental car airport kiosk and the other clutching a to-go cup of lukewarm coffee. "Irish roads are known for being narrow."

"I don't think we're actually on the road anymore," Fern said as he raised his head from where he'd been resting it against the window, his travel pillow still hugging his neck. "Not on my side at least."

I glanced out to see that the stone wall we'd come so close to grazing had been replaced by tall grass slapping the window. The broken yellow line that marked the edge of the road was nowhere to be seen. We were, indeed, driving on the shoulder. Not that I blamed Richard. The only person I could blame for getting us into this situation was myself.

As the owner of Wedding Belles, Washington DC's premiere wedding planning firm, I'd been only too eager to jump at the chance to work with a U.S. senator's daughter on her upcoming wedding to a Silicon Valley tycoon. I'd been even more thrilled when she'd decided on a destination wedding, since I'd been hoping to expand the Wedding Belles reach overseas, and been delighted she'd settled on Ireland as her destination. An English-speaking country only a six-hour hop across the pond seemed the perfect place to get our feet wet with international weddings.

What I hadn't thought about was the fact that most cars in the country were manual transmission, which I didn't drive, and barely large enough to fit one suitcase in the tiny trunks, let alone four. My assistant, Kate, and I had been excited that our client wanted to send the entire design team over to Ireland to scout out potential venues, but now we were barreling down an Irish highway with a pile of suitcases strapped precariously to the roof and both Fern's and Richard's designer carry-on bags stacked between Kate and Fern in the back seat.

Kate peeked over the Louis Vuitton and Gucci wall. "I'd rather be on the grass side than the car side."

"If you think you can do a better job, you're more than welcome to come up and try," Richard said.

"No," Fern and I said in unison. Kate wasn't a great driver to begin with, so I could only imagine how bad she'd be driving on the opposite side of the road and trying to shift with her left hand.

Kate mumbled something and flopped back in her seat. I took a sip of my watery coffee, grimaced, and made the decision to drink tea for the rest of the trip as I dropped the coffee into the console's cup holder.

"Do I even need to say aloud how much you owe me for this,

darling?" Richard asked, flicking his eyes to me then quickly back to the road as a box truck rumbled within inches of our car, and we both flinched. "If I start to perspire from stress, this silk cardigan is ruined."

I glanced at his simple, yet no doubt pricey, gray sweater. "I'll buy you a new one."

"You can't afford it," he said.

That was probably true. Richard didn't find it unusual to spend more on an item of clothing than I did on rent, and he made no secret that he thought my off-the-rack habits were a serious character flaw. It was one he was willing to overlook since I sent him so much business and since we'd been best friends since I'd moved to DC several years earlier.

I tried to ease my foot off the floor where I'd been ghost braking for the past hour. "I thought you were pleased I got you added to the Wedding Belles team as our culinary consultant. The client is paying you handsomely to work with the chef at whichever venue we select so the food is up to his standards."

By "his" I meant the senator, our bride's father, who was well known in Washington as a food and wine connoisseur. Since Richard was the owner of the renowned Richard Gerard Catering firm and had done parties for the senator and his wife, it hadn't been a hard sell, but I didn't want my best friend to know that. I'd learned long ago that it paid to keep Richard a little humble, if that was at all possible.

"When you mentioned a destination wedding in Ireland, I didn't envision a clown car filled with vendors and myself at the wheel," he muttered.

"It could be worse," Kate said. "Buster and Mack could have flown over with us."

Richard's eyes widened. "Perish the thought. We would have had to strap them to the bumper."

"Not when they're bigger than the car we wouldn't," I reminded him as I turned the map and my elbow bumped his.

My go-to floral team consisted of two men who'd left husky

in the rearview mirror, wore black leather with chains, and rode Harleys. Luckily, they'd had a big floral order to take care of in DC and would be flying over later to join us. I hadn't worked out where we'd put them when they arrived, but I still had time.

"How much longer until we're there?" Fern asked, yawning and tightening his dark man bun.

Richard glared at him in the rearview mirror. "Remind me again why we needed a hairstylist on a scouting trip."

"He's my plus one," Kate said, her head appearing between us again.

"This isn't a date function." Richard mumbled something about millennials and their life expectations under his breath. "This is work. We need to do site visits of as many luxury castles and manors as we can in a short time frame, which means no dillydallying."

Fern patted him on the shoulder. "Don't get your knickers in a twist, sweetie. I'm totally focused on venues. Not to mention I've been doing Hailey's hair for years, so I'm familiar with her taste."

Hailey was our bride, and Fern—short for Fernando because his mother had been an ABBA groupie—was the reason she'd learned about Wedding Belles in the first place, so I had no problem with him joining us. I knew deep down Richard didn't either, but the driving was getting to him.

"It shouldn't be long now," I said, glancing at a sign and back down at our map. "We left the Shannon airport almost an hour ago, so we should be to Adare soon."

The congestion of the airport area had given way to green stretches of land with the occasional rolling hill, but we had yet to see sheep or cliffs or charming cottages that defined Ireland in my head.

Fern stretched his arms over his head and they hit the ceiling. "I don't know about you, but I'm ready for a nap."

"You didn't get any sleep on the plane?" I asked, tucking a long strand of hair back behind my ear. Sleeping on planes didn't come easily to me, but I'd managed to get a few hours despite Kate slumped against my shoulder.

I twisted my head to see that Fern still had the kelly-green cashmere scarf he'd used as an airplane blanket wrapped around his neck. He'd presented us each with one before takeoff, claiming it would improve our team unity and morale for the trip. I wasn't sure about that, but mine had been a welcome layer on the chilly flight.

I eyed the scarf topping his black turtleneck. Since Fern usually went to great lengths to match his outfits according to the season, holiday, or color scheme, I was grateful he wasn't decked out in full leprechaun gear. Of course I hadn't gotten a peek inside his luggage, and the day was young.

"I went through my skin care travel regimen and even had my sheet mask on," Fern said, "but then I started talking with the cute couple across the aisle."

“Wearing a sheet mask, you spent six hours talking to people?” I asked.

He giggled. "Can you believe it? But my skin is as soft as a baby's bottom." He touched his fingertips to his cheeks. "Want to feel?"

I shook my head. "I'm good. So what was the deal with the couple?" I vaguely remembered a perky blonde and a nondescript guy.

"Honeymooners." Fern clapped his hands. "Isn't that sweet? They're doing a tour of Ireland just like we are."

"Ugh," Kate said. "I'm glad I slept through that."

I was with Kate, although I might not have said it out loud. After spending nearly every day of the year with brides and grooms, the last thing I wanted to encounter on a trip was a pair of newlyweds. They were inevitably coming off the high of their wedding and could talk of nothing else.

"Probably not just like us," I said, "unless they plan to tour ballrooms and meet with chefs."

"No," Fern admitted, "but I did tell them all the places we

were going since you'd done all the research to find the most romantic castles in the country."

Kate swung her head around. "Are you telling me we might have honeymooners on our trail for the entire trip?"

Fern swatted at her over the pile of bags. "Of course not. You know how people are with advice. They never take it even if they ask for it. But I wouldn't be unhappy to see them again." He leaned forward and dropped his voice to a whisper. "P.S. Annabelle, I'll need another itinerary."

"The only reason you care about seeing them again is so you can get your hands on the woman's hair, isn't it?" Kate asked.

Fern sucked in a breath. "What an outrageous accusation." He turned his head to the window and looked over his shoulder. "Maybe just to shape it. These girls grow it out for their weddings and then it just hangs there." He wrinkled his nose. "You know I can't see problems in this world without wanting to fix them."

I tried not to roll my eyes. "You're a one-man Gates Foundation all right. I might have an extra itinerary, but remember, we're here to find Hailey's dream wedding spot, and we have less than a week in which to do it."

"I'm still surprised the bride didn't want to do this," Kate said.

"She can't exactly study for the bar exam and go gallivanting around Ireland," I said. "I promised to send her lots of photos along the way."

"Don't worry about me, Annabelle." Fern patted my shoulder. "I'm completely focused on the wedding." He gasped. "Sheep! Look at all the sheep!"

A verdant hill stretched up to our right with the fluffy creatures nibbling lazily on the green grass. A stone wall intersected the hill with the worn stones stacked tightly together.

"Can we stop and pet them?" Kate asked, pointing through the glass. "Look, there's even a little one."

"No sheep." Richard waved a finger in the air. "This is exactly the distraction Annabelle was talking about."

Both Fern and Kate grumbled in the back seat.

"This is it." I pointed ahead as a pair of stone gateposts came into view with black lanterns attached to the front and decorative stone urns on top. I squinted at the brass nameplates on each pillar that read "Adare Manor" and felt my stomach flutter when I realized we'd arrived at the five-star resort and golf club.

We all leaned forward as Richard slowly turned the car into the drive, and an attendant in a gold-braided uniform and top hat checked our names off a list and waved us through. As we curved around the long driveway and the massive stone manor came into view, with turrets rising high and green ivy covering its walls, my jaw dropped. Manicured gardens stretched in front of us leading up to the manor house, and I noticed a thick forest surrounding the historic house.

Kate rolled down her window and poked her head out for a better view. "Blimey."

2

"It's like Downton Abbey," Fern said, his face pressed to the car window as we drove alongside hedgerows and tall squared-off boxwoods as we approached the manor house.

"Are those words carved into the building?" Kate asked, pointing to Gothic letters that appeared to be chiseled into the stone atop the roof.

I narrowed my eyes to read them, but could only make out the phrase "build the house" before we were driving past the manor and around the side.

Fern gasped as the house extended further to the back. "Do you think the servants will wear full livery and bow to us?"

"I hope not," I said. "This is the twenty-first century, and you are a hotel guest, not the lord of the manor."

Fern sniffed, pulling the elastic from the bun on top of his head and letting his brown hair fall around his shoulders. "I hope you're not implying I'm the *lady* of the manor."

"Take the fifth, Annabelle," Richard said under his breath.

Once Richard had pulled into a small parking area, I opened the car door and stretched my legs in front of me, grateful to extend them after being wedged into a Peugeot for the past hour and a plane for the six hours before that. "I'm implying you're an American who's not 'of the manor' in any form."

Fern joined me outside the car and shielded his eyes as he peered up at the house. "Give me time, sweetie."

The gray stone mansion looked even larger from the back with a covered stone walkway leading from the main building to a wing that was clearly newer but designed in the same Gothic style. Rows of high arched windows extended up between the two tall turrets of the entrance, which was set off to the left instead of the center of the building, and elaborate scroll work adorned the edifice.

A man in a long gray coat with gold buttons and a top hat approached the car, eyeing our stack of suitcases strapped on top.

Richard glanced at his brass name tag. "Good morning, Dermot. We're checking in."

"Welcome to Adare Manor," the white-bearded man said, a slight lilt in his accent. "Go along inside, and we'll take care of your luggage."

Richard handed him the keys and palmed him a few Euros. "I understand if you need to hide this squat little thing somewhere out of view."

I was about to ask which of us he was calling squat when I looked around us, saw the row of luxury cars lined up on the paving stones, and realized he was referring to our rental car.

Fern tossed the end of his scarf over his shoulder, hooked his Louis Vuitton duffel over the crook of his arm, and extended his other arm to Kate. "Shall we, my dear?"

Kate fluffed her fingers through her bob and straightened her pink sheath, and the two walked ahead through the stone archway. How did those two look good enough to walk the red carpet, and I looked like I'd slept in my clothes, which I had? I still couldn't believe Kate had worn a dress on the plane and that it looked as good as it did. I'd worn black jeans and a dove-gray hooded tunic and felt like I'd gathered every crumb and piece of lint in the entire plane. I brushed off my pants, hoping I looked presentable enough to check in.

"Coming, darling?" Richard asked, pausing as he slung his black Gucci man bag across his shoulder.

I pulled out the folder with our itinerary and reservation confirmations as I followed him inside the hotel, stopping once we'd reached the lobby so I could soak in the atmosphere and adjust to the noise level.

Stone columns soared up two stories with a crystal chandelier hanging between them, and a wood balcony jutted out over one side of the impressive hall. Rich burgundy carpet covered the floor, and a massive black granite hearth dominated one wall. Gilded mirrors and antler heads were in abundance, and a baby grand piano sat in the center of the room, its ebony surface shining. I pulled out my phone, stepping back to get a good wide angle shot to send the bride.

"It's very Old World," Richard said. Considering how fond he was of clean lines, I wasn't sure if this was a good or bad thing.

"It is almost two hundred years old." I took a photo of the towering peaked windows streaming midmorning light into the room and dropped my phone back into my bag. My awe at the intricate detailing of the room was only slightly overshadowed by the large chattering tour group clustered around a mahogany reception desk.

"Americans," Richard whispered to me with some amount of disdain as he appraised the all-female group that seemed to consist of mostly gray heads.

"We're Americans," I reminded him.

"Yes, but we're not wearing leisure suits and sweatshirts with pithy sayings." He clutched my arm as a woman with silver hair and a sweatshirt that read "Don't Mess with Grandma" walked past us. "You don't think Leatrice is in this group, do you? They look like her people."

"Calm down," I told him. "She's at home with Sidney Allen, looking after your dog, remember?"

His fingers relaxed their grip. "Of course. Silly me. I think the flight and the driving have addled my brain."

My downstairs neighbor, Leatrice, loved eccentric clothing, surveilling her neighbors, and taking care of Richard's Yorkie, Hermès. She'd recently become engaged to an equally quirky entertainment coordinator I worked with, and both were most likely home in our Georgetown apartment building planning her wedding, watching vintage TV, and spoiling Hermès.

Richard glanced at his watch. "Do you think it's too early for me to call and check on him?"

After insisting most of his life that pets and children were too messy and unpredictable for him, he'd acquired Hermès when a casual dating situation had morphed into something more, and the pint-sized pup was part of the package. Unfortunately, Richard's significant other traveled for the State Department, so Richard had assumed the lion's share of the pet care. After some initial complaints and a generous amount of hand sanitizer, he'd taken to carrying the dog everywhere with him in his man bag. Now Richard and Hermès owned matching Burberry jackets and plaid pajamas.

I made a quick mental calculation. "Only if you consider four in the morning to be too early."

"I'll wait. I'm sure he's fine."

I patted his arm. "He and Leatrice probably stayed up late watching old noir movies and doing their nails."

"Are we talking about my dog or Sidney Allen?"

I shrugged, noticing the doorman deposit our luggage next to two brass bell carts stacked high with suitcases. "Take your pick."

"Guess what," Fern said, rushing up dragging Kate behind him. "I just met the nicest ladies."

Richard raised an eyebrow. "You mean the sweatpants grandmas?"

Fern swatted at him. "Be nice. They aren't all in sweatpants and they aren't all grandmas." He tapped a finger to his chin. "Actually, I don't know if they all are or not. The good news is they didn't bring grandchildren if they have them. They're here from the U.S. on a genealogical tour. They're tracking down their Irish roots. Isn't that exciting?"

"This is a pretty upscale place for a tour group," I said, remembering how much the senator was paying for each of our rooms.

"I think most of them must have money from dead husbands," Fern said, his voice low. "I recognize the look of well-heeled widows."

Richard didn't look so convinced. "Well-heeled widows in sweats?"

"Don't look at the clothes. They just came off the plane like we did." He cut his eyes to a woman in a yellow velour track suit. "Focus on the fingers and the handbags."

I cut my eyes to the woman and noticed a huge diamond ring and the interlocking Cs of the Chanel logo on her black quilted bag. So not your typical traveling grandmas.

"I didn't see a tour bus outside," I said.

Fern wrinkled his nose. "This is a custom tour, so they have one of those fancy minibuses with a driver. Apparently the lady with the Dowager Countess hairdo arranged it all."

I followed his gaze to a woman with steel gray hair piled on top of her head and a black binder in her hands. Unlike most of the other ladies, she did not wear sweats, but instead had on a wrinkle-free beige pantsuit.

"Myrna heads up the online group as well," Fern explained.

"Online?" Richard asked. "Don't tell me they're wannabe hackers like Leatrice."

"You know she gave that up," I said, not wanting to dwell on my neighbor's brief foray into the underbelly of the internet.

"That's how they met," Fern said, giving one of the women a

finger wave. "They're in a Facebook group for widows looking for Irish ancestors."

Kate tilted her head at him. "How specific."

Fern fluttered a hand. "There's a group for everything these days. Don't ask me how, but I'm in a group for man bun aficionados. Of course, it's mostly women posting pictures of Jason Momoa."

"That's what most Facebook groups are these days," Kate said, "and I, for one, am fine with it."

I rubbed my head, feeling the exhaustion from the long night in the airplane setting in. "You know a lot about these ladies." I leaned in to Richard. "How much of a head start did these two get in here?"

Richard patted my hand. "You know Fern. He can make friends with a potted palm."

"Comes with the hairstylist territory." Fern winked at me. "People seem to confess their souls around me."

The woman Fern had identified as Myrna raised her voice as she shuffled her group out of the lobby. "Back down here by one o'clock for falconry, ladies."

"Falconry?" Richard's eyes widened. "There are falcons here?"

"I think so." I hiked my tote higher on my shoulder and moved toward the open reception desk. "You have an issue with falcons?"

"Animals with razor-sharp talons?" He shuddered. "Sounds charming, but no, thank you."

""It took him months to acclimate to a five-pound dog, Annabelle," Kate said. "I wouldn't hold my breath for falcons."

As I greeted the woman at the reception desk and handed her our confirmations, my phone began vibrating. I pulled it out of my bag and glanced at the screen, feeling myself smile when I saw my boyfriend's name pop up.

"It's Reese," I said, handing my bag to Kate. "Can you get us checked in while I take this?"

Kate wagged her eyebrows at me. "Tell hot cop I said hi."

I gave Kate a look. I wasn't crazy about her referring to my boyfriend as hot cop, even though he was a DC cop, a detective actually, and he was hot. I still had a hard time believing a hard-bodied, dark-haired detective had picked a workaholic wedding planner who wore a perpetual ponytail and considered wedding cake one of her food groups.

I took a few steps away as I answered. "You have good timing. We just arrived at our hotel. Do you miss me already?"

"Annabelle," my boyfriend said. "I need you to get on the next plane back home."

3

"You're kidding, right?" I asked, my heart thudding in my chest.

He let out a resigned sigh on the other end. "Yes, but I had no idea how much time Sidney Allen would spend in our apartment."

"Sidney Allen? As in Leatrice's fiancé?"

"I'm not sure if it's Leatrice that's getting to him, or Leatrice's wedding planning, or Leatrice's weird relationship with Richard's dog, but he showed up at our door after you left and ended up watching ESPN with me until I kicked him out after midnight."

I scratched my head. "Sidney Allen watched sports?"

It made sense that he wanted a break from Leatrice. What didn't make sense was the excitable entertainment guru watching sports. From what I knew of him, the small egg-shaped man walked around events with a headset and directed his costumed performers like a ground crew waved in airplanes. Sidney Allen was the person you called when you wanted to recreate Cirque de Soleil in your backyard or have a Renaissance-themed party complete with court jesters and bawdy serving wenches. He lived in dark suits, hiked his pants almost to his armpits, and gave Richard a run for his money when it came to overreacting. He did not lounge around, and he certainly didn't watch ESPN.

"Unless I was hallucinating," Reese said. "Which is entirely possible considering how wiped I was after pulling a double shift. But I'm pretty sure he mentioned dropping by again tonight. If this is going to be a regular occurrence, I may have to hop on the next plane to Ireland and join you."

Kate handed me a small paper room key folder. I watched her hand similar ones to Fern and Richard then motion to me that they were going upstairs. I nodded and followed behind, ducking as Fern tossed his green scarf over his shoulder.

"You want to ride around in a car with the four of us?" I asked as we headed up a mahogany staircase. I let Richard walk a few steps ahead of me before dropping my voice. "Richard's driving."

"Maybe not. I guess I'll just have to pull longer shifts while you're gone or do a better job of sneaking into our apartment building."

"My best tips for that are taking off your shoes and making sure the front door doesn't slam behind you on the first floor."

Reese laughed. "So you're saying I need to be a cat burglar to get into my own apartment?"

"Pretty much," I said as we walked down a long corridor and read room numbers as we went. "I've been doing it for years so Leatrice wouldn't know I was home."

"I didn't think it worked all that well," Reese said.

"I didn't say it was foolproof. Leatrice has supersonic hearing for an eighty year old, but if you're lucky, Sidney Allen doesn't." I hoisted my black Longchamp tote bag onto my shoulder as it slipped down. "You could always turn off all the lights and hide under the bed."

"Leatrice bothering him?" Kate whispered, turning around.

I covered the bottom of the phone and shook my head. "Sidney Allen."

Kate's eyebrows popped up. "I'm not sure if that's better or worse."

"Worse," Richard said from a few paces ahead where he'd stopped in front of a dark wood door. "At least the old dear has good taste when it comes to dogs." He opened the door and pushed it open. "I'm going to freshen up and check in with Hermès. I'll see you all later."

"I'm across from you, Annabelle," Kate said, flashing her room key at me.

I gave her a small wave and watched her disappear inside her room, and then I opened my own door and pushed it open with one hip. "Wow."

"I hope you're saying that about the views and not about the Irish lads," Reese said.

"Funny." I took a few steps into the room and dropped my bag on the dark-blue love seat tucked at the foot of the king - sized bed. "My room is gorgeous."

Even though it wasn't enormous, the ceilings were high and a crystal chandelier hung from the center. A trio of windows took up the far wall and overlooked a river bank edged with trees. Cream-colored curtains hung from floor to ceiling and were the same soft shade as the damask wallpaper. The bed and the tables--from the nightstands to the low coffee table--were dark wood with the crisp white duvet and a pile of fluffy pillows a sharp contrast. Over the bed hung a tapestry in soft blues and dusty rose--a medieval scene of lords and ladies alongside horses and the curved bows of ships.

"Hold on," I said, pressing the camera app on my phone. "I should take some photos to show the bride since these are the rooms her guests would get."

I snapped a few shots then walked into the bathroom, trying not to gasp out loud. A glass standing shower was the first thing I saw, but my eyes were immediately drawn to the tall windows above a freestanding soaking tub, letting light stream into the room. A pair of mirrors perched over the gray marble double vanity, and high-end toiletries stood in a yellow row between the two sinks.

I took a few more pictures before holding the phone to my ear again. "You don't mind if I talk to you while I take a bath, do you?"

He chuckled. "I'm assuming the bathroom there is better than ours?"

"You assume correctly." I loved a lot of things about my older stone-front apartment building in Georgetown. The dated bathrooms were not one of them.

I twisted the shiny chrome handle and the tub began filling with water. After examining the Acqua di Parma toiletries, I plucked the mango-yellow tube of bath and shower gel off the counter and squeezed some under the rushing water. The perfumed scent began to fill the room, and I felt the knots in my shoulders start to unravel.

"Isn't it still really early in DC?" I asked, stepping a few steps away from the noise of the running water, peeling off my black jeans, and tucking them into one of the open cubbies under the sink that held white towels.

"I have to be in early again." Reese yawned loudly. "We're wrapping up a murder investigation."

"The romance author who killed her husband?" I asked as I pulled my tunic over my head and wrapped a towel around me before taking off my underwear. I looked out the windows overlooking the green lawn, not seeing anyone, but not relishing the thought of stripping naked in front of an open window either.

"Yep. The case is pretty tight, especially since she wrote about a woman who got revenge on a cheating husband in one of her books."

"What was the murder weapon?" I held my hand under the water to test the temperature.

"Nice try, babe."

"What?" I flipped off the water, stepped into the tub, and let myself sink into the warm water, dropping the towel to the floor once I was below the windowsill.

"You're in Ireland to research castles and fancy houses for a wedding. You're not supposed to be thinking about my murder case."

"Sorry." I let my head rest on the curved lip of the tub and stretched out my legs. "Old habits die hard."

I rolled my head to one side and could just see out the window where a group was walking across the lawn. From the brightly colored outfits, it looked like the genealogy grandmas. As I rotated my head forward, a vivid green flash caught my eye. I sat up higher. Was that Fern with them?

"You've got to be kidding me," I muttered.

"What?"

"Not you." I slid back down under the bubbles. "Fern made fast friends with some elderly American women here to hunt down their Irish roots, and it looks like he's tagged along on their falconry experience."

"That sounds about right. Has Kate fallen in love already and Richard had a nervous breakdown?"

I laughed. He knew my friends too well. "To answer your questions--as to Kate, not yet, but give it a few hours, and regarding Richard's nervous breakdown, of course."

He chuckled. "I know it's work, but promise me you'll have some fun while you're there. Drink some Guinness, kiss the Blarney Stone, and eat lots of soda bread."

I switched the phone to my other ear. "Did you read up on things to do in Ireland?"

"I might have." He cleared his throat. "The more you talked about it, the more I thought it would be the kind of place I'd like to visit with you one day."

I felt a warmth spread through my body that had nothing to do with the water in the tub. "That's so sweet. We've never really traveled together before, except for the time you flew halfway across the world to help me catch a killer."

"Not exactly the most romantic trip."

"I don't know." I sank lower in the tub so the bubbles from the bath gel reached my neck. "I had a good time once you got there. You're right, though. Ireland is the perfect place for a relaxing getaway."

"What about for a honeymoon?"

I nearly dropped the phone into the water as I slipped down, my feet flying up and the back of my head falling into the water. I yelped and grabbed the side of the tub for balance, holding my phone up high with the other.

"Annabelle? Babe, are you still there?"

"I'm here," I said, coughing and sitting up. "Just slipped a bit."

"You're sure I didn't freak you out?"

"Me? Freak out?" I laughed, but it sounded too high and too fake. "I plan weddings for a living. Why would the mention of a honeymoon make me nervous?"

"We've never really talked about it before. Marriage, I mean."

I steadied my breath and hoped my slower breathing would also steady my racing heart. "You're right. We haven't." Were we really having this discussion when I was thousands of miles away and naked?

"Annie?" Kate's voice made me swing my head toward the open bathroom door.

You have got to be kidding me, I thought as my assistant walked into the bathroom.

"You have a tub too," she said, nodding and smiling as she took in the room. "But your view is better than mine."

She came closer, and I slipped back down under the water. "Do you mind?"

She glanced at my phone and put a hand over her mouth. "Sorry. Still talking with Reese?"

Before I could wave her out so I could get back to my boyfriend and his bombshell, Richard barreled into the room. "Here you both are."

He spun on his heel when he saw me in the tub, glanced over at Kate, and then shook his head. "I've been saying for years you two need to set professional boundaries."

“How did you both waltz into my room?” I asked.

Kate hopped up onto the marble countertop. “I got us each copies of each other’s room keys. Didn’t you see them in the back of the key card folder I gave you?”

That was the last time I let Kate check us in, I thought. No way did I want to spend a week in Ireland with my friends walking into my room at all hours.

"What is it?" I asked Richard, trying not to grit my teeth or scream. He faced away from me with his hands on his hips.

"It's a disaster is what it is." Richard threw his hands into the air. "Everything is ruined."

4

"Just so we're clear," I said as I settled into the passenger seat of our rental car, "Leatrice feeding Hermès Milk Bones does not constitute an emergency."

Richard gave me a look that told me he clearly disagreed. "It does when I've spent ages training him to like the organic dog biscuits our chef makes for him."

"Wait a second," Kate said as she got into the back seat. "You have your chef make dog biscuits for you?"

Richard eyed her as he adjusted the rearview mirror. "I can't exactly have a chef from another catering company make them. It's a proprietary recipe that took me months to develop."

"For dog biscuits?" I said, emphasizing each word and hoping he would pick up on how ridiculous I thought it was.

"Yes, Annabelle." Richard spoke slowly as well, as if talking to a small child, and he patted my hand. "That *is* what we're talking about. Try to keep up, darling."

I cut my eyes to him as he put the keys into the ignition. I was still steamed at him for barging into my bath and interrupting my conversation with Reese, even if a part of me felt relieved not to have to deal with the topic my boyfriend had introduced. By the time I'd shooed everyone out of my bathroom, Reese had had to head off to work and my bubbles had disappeared. I couldn't blame Kate and Richard entirely. I'd clammed up at the mention of the "M" word. Despite the fact that I planned weddings for a living, I hadn't spent too much time thinking about if or when I'd actually tie the knot.

The sad fact of my job was that, until recently, it had kept me too busy to date. Not that I'd met many eligible bachelors. The grooms were taken, and the groomsmen I'd always considered off-limits. If I hadn't had so many unfortunate incidents at weddings, I might never have met Detective Mike Reese. Our romance hadn't enjoyed the smoothest path, and Richard had taken a while to accept the fact that I had another man in my life. It had been nearly six months since Reese had moved in with me, and I felt like things had only recently gotten into an easy rhythm. The idea of taking things to the next level so soon made my stomach do somersaults. Add that to the fact that all the women I knew who were engaged--aka my clients--also became a little crazy, and the thought of being one of those women made me want to run for the hills.

I rolled down the car window and inhaled the scent of grass and impending rain, looking up at the gray clouds in the distance. "We'd better get to the village before the rain comes."

Richard drummed his fingers on the steering wheel. "Fern did know what time we were leaving for dinner, right?"

"I slipped a note under his door," Kate said, shrugging her kelly-green cashmere wrap over her shoulders.

I glanced at the lush lawn of the estate. "Let's hope he went back to his room to see it. I told you I saw him outside with the genealogy ladies, right?"

Richard snapped his head to face me. "He's taken up with another group?"

"I wouldn't say 'taken up.' It looked like he was joining them for their falconry lesson, although I didn't watch long enough to see the birds." I shot Kate a look. "Someone came in and distracted me."

She gave me an arch smile in return. "Oh, I think you were already pretty distracted talking to your honey."

I felt my face flush as I turned back around. No way was I going to tell Kate--or anyone--what had come up when I'd been on the phone with Reese. It would send everyone into a frenzy and would confuse me even more. I rubbed my clammy hands on the front of my jeans and spotted Fern rushing out of the manor, the long ends of his scarf flying behind him and giving him the look of an Irish ace pilot.

"Sorry I'm late, dolls." He was out of breath as he slid into the back seat.

We all took a moment to take in his attire--brown tweed pants that narrowed at the ankle and a matching snug fitting jacket, a hunter-green tweed vest peeking out from under the three-button jacket, and a flat-topped tweed cap. He unwound his green scarf from his neck.

"What?" he touched a hand to his lapel. "I didn't have time to change after the falconry."

I knew how much effort Fern put into his outfits. "You look very . . ."

"Irish?" he asked.

"Tweedy," Richard said, pressing the gas and jolting us out of the parking space.

Fern gave Kate an appreciative look and touched the green scarf he'd given her. "At least someone else is getting into the spirit of the trip." He leaned his head between the front seats. "Unlike some people I could mention."

"I promise I'll wear my scarf the next time we go out," I said. "I was in a rush to get dressed this time, not to mention to get everyone out of my room."

He slumped back on his seat. "Did I miss a party in Annabelle's room?"

"No!" I said, more forcefully than I'd intended. "But we did see you heading out with the ladies."

"How were the falcons?" Kate asked once we were driving down the long lane leading away from the hotel.

"Magnificent," Fern said. "But my favorites were the owls. They have a snowy one that looked stunning with my coloring. I'm thinking of getting one when we get back home."

"An owl?" Richard asked as he eased the car onto the main road leading into the village of Adare. "You're thinking of getting an owl?"

Fern nodded. "You carry a dog around in your man bag. Why can't I carry an owl around on my shoulder?"

Great. Just what we needed--to be a walking menagerie.

As Richard muttered something about the difference between carrying a dog and an owl, I pointed at an oncoming car. "Don't forget we're supposed to be on the left."

He swerved the car and we all lurched to one side. "They really need to make these roads wider."

"I'm sure the country of Ireland will get right on that," Kate said.

I ignored Richard's snarky response as we entered the village proper and passed a series of thatched roof cottages--some covered in moss, some whitewashed, and others stone fronted. A waist-high stone wall ran the length of the row of houses, and signs hung from posts in front of some indicating they were restaurants.

"Charming," Fern said. "Aside from all the tourists crowding the sidewalks and taking pictures."

I flipped open the Ireland guidebook Richard had tucked into the center console, reading as we drove. "Adare has been called the prettiest village in Ireland and has been named a Tidy Town by the government."

"Tidy Towns. Now that's a concept I can get behind." Richard nodded his head as we approached what looked like the main business district with rows of two-story buildings abutting one another.

Colorful with fat chimneys, the shops and restaurants had Irish flags and hanging baskets of flowers in front. We slowed with the traffic, and I spotted a black-and-white building ahead at the juncture where the road divided. It drew my eye with a double gabled roof, dormer windows on each side, and a red doorway.

"I wonder what that is?" I said aloud, skimming my guidebook, but finding no information.

"What is?" Richard glanced over at me, and the car drifted closer to the middle.

"Left!" Kate screamed from behind us, and Richard jerked the car back in line as an oncoming car swiped his side view mirror, and it spun into the air and flew behind us.

Richard slammed on the brakes. "That's it. I'm done with driving." He jerked the car into park in the middle of the street and opened his door.

"What are you doing?" I leaned over the center console as he stepped out of the car. "Don't worry about the mirror. We got the extra insurance."

Kate looked behind us at the line of cars approaching. "I mean, I've done some bad parking in my day, but this takes the cape."

Fern cocked his head, no doubt working the mangled phrase over in his head to see if it was right.

"You mean cake," I said. "Takes the cake."

Kate shrugged. "Sure, that too."

"Richard," I called as he stood with his hand on the doorframe, "we can't stay here in the middle of the road."

Kate opened her door. "I'll find the mirror while you talk him off the ledge."

Talking Richard off the ledge had become a specialty of mine over the years, and I liked to think it honed my skills for calming down nervous brides. I watched Kate give the cars behind us an exuberant wave as she bobbed her way between them, ducking her head down to get a better view of the ground. I didn't hear any honks of complaints and chalked it up to the more polite and laid-back Irish people. It probably didn't hurt that she was very blond and her skirt was very short.

"It's fine," I told Richard as I stepped out of my side of the car. "You're doing great. I'm sure this kind of thing happens all the time here."

"Found it!" Kate yelled from a few cars back as she held up the intact side view mirror.

"See?" I said. "No biggie."

Richard crossed his arms. "And what are we supposed to do with it now that it isn't attached to the car? Am I supposed to drive while holding it out the window with one hand?"

Fern joined us outside the car. "Do you think you could do that?"

Richard narrowed his eyes at him.

"Let's not worry about this now," I said as Kate jogged back to the car with the mirror in hand. "If we park the car, we can have a nice dinner somewhere and figure out our next steps."

"You're right," Fern said, twisting his neck to scan the street. "There's a pub right there that looks pinch-me cute. A couple of pints of Guinness, and we'll all feel better."

Richard straightened his shoulders. "If you think beer will improve my mood, you don't know me at all."

"Come on, Richard," I said, hearing the pleading tone in my own voice. "Get back in the car. You're the only one who can drive it."

"Not technically true," Kate said when she reached us. "I can drive stick."

Fern, Richard, and I all exchanged a glance.

Kate strode up to the driver's side, nudged Richard out of the way, and tossed the mirror into the back seat. "Hop in if you don't want to sit here all day." She plopped herself in front of the steering wheel, slammed the door shut, and revved the engine.

Fern disappeared back into the car before I could decide, and the car lurched forward, leaving Richard and me standing in the middle of the road. I watched open-mouthed as Kate careened to the end of the street, made a tight U-turn, and angled into a barely legal space.

"You are officially not allowed to read any more books about how to empower your employees." Richard scurried over to the sidewalk with me.

"It was one book," I said as we walked to the car. "But point taken."

Fern stood on the sidewalk looking up at the marine-blue pub with wide white windows and bright-red signs announcing that Pat Collins Bar had fine food and drink. "This looks as good as any." He squinted his eyes at the specials written in chalk on the slate board next to the door. "I think the Irish stew would go best with my outfit, don't you?"

"Definitely," Kate said.

I hooked my arm through Richard's. "I promise you'll feel better once we eat."

He squeezed my hand. "You're probably right. The last food I had was on the plane, and you know how irritable processed food makes me."

Fern sucked in his breath as he peered into one of the pub's multipaned windows. "I don't believe it." His face broke into a grin. "The ladies from the hotel are inside. Let's go see if we can join them."

Richard groaned as Fern threw open the shiny black door. "I'm in hell."

Kate winked at us as she followed him. "At least hell serves pints."

5

"Isn't this fun?" Fen asked as we squeezed into a long upholstered banquette that ran along the back of the pub and was fronted with low polished wood tables in an assortment of shapes and sizes.

The ladies from the genealogical tour had been more than happy to add us to their group when Fern had burst into the pub like he was one of the long-lost relatives they were searching for. I tried to smile as I wedged myself next to a gray-haired woman who wore a bright-green fanny pack around her waist facing front, and a beige security wallet— meant to be tucked under clothing—around her neck and on top of her purple blouse. Richard dragged an unused chair from another table and plopped it across from me at the small round table, giving me a self-satisfied grin. I knew he was pleased that he'd managed not to be body-to-body with people he didn't know, and I suppressed the urge to kick him under the table.

I waved at Kate and Fern at the other end of the long banquette, but both were deep in conversation with ladies from the group. The chatter from the ten or so women plus our four added to the low hum of the full pub. It wasn't loud enough to need to shout, but between the dinner guests, the people bellied up to the bar, and the televisions playing a European football match, it was far from quiet.

Although bustling with activity, the pub felt cozy with none of the high-ceilinged grandeur of our hotel. Light came in from the large windows, but the carpet and furniture were dark blue and the heavy drapes a rich shade of crimson. The wooden bar greeted you as you entered and curved around the room with stools lined up along it and bottles arranged in rows behind the busy bartenders. The scent of beer and baking bread seemed to hang in the air and made me want to breathe in deeply.

"Fernando told us you were all from our nation's capital," the woman with the fanny pack said, holding out a hand. "I'm Colleen. From Cincinnati."

It was rare I heard Fern referred to by his full name—he tired of explaining his mother's passion for ABBA when he gave it—but if anyone would insist on calling him by his proper name, I suspected it would be a group of grandmothers.

"Annabelle," I said. "From Washington. And my smug friend is Richard."

Richard extended his fingertips. "Charmed."

"And I'm Betty Belle from Amarillo, Texas." The woman on my other side had hair spun up around her head like a cotton candy halo of white and wore a Texas flag lapel pin.

"So you're really from all over the country?" I asked as a waitress appeared and eyed our group.

The woman I recognized as Myrna suggested a round of Guinness since it was everyone's first night in Ireland, and the waitress hurried off again, no doubt glad she didn't have to take a complicated drink order.

"From sea to shining sea," Betty Belle said, winking at me. "We'd never have known each other if it weren't for Myrna. She's helped all of us track down our Irish connections."

Colleen nodded. "Of course some of us have become friends through the group and during previous trips."

Richard leaned forward. "This isn't your first time?"

"Myrna brings a group every year. Mostly new people, but some repeats." Colleen pointed halfway down the banquette to a woman wearing a wildly colorful peasant blouse and red hair that could only be produced from a bottle. "This is Nancy's third trip."

"She's found all her ancestors," Betty Belle said in a stage whisper. "I think she keeps coming for the beer."

"Or the bread," Colleen said, sucking in a long breath. "She wouldn't stop talking about the brown bread the entire flight over."

As if on cue, our waitress reappeared with plates stacked high with thick slices of brown bread. Myrna leaned down the table, her voice raised. "I asked for some bread to start us out."

Hands dove for the bread and the small gold-wrapped squares of butter. I even saw Fern slathering a piece despite being an off-and-on devotee of the Keto diet. When in Rome, I supposed. Or Ireland.

"Why are you four in Ireland?" Colleen asked after swallowing.

I spread butter on a small rectangle of bread, trying to keep it from crumbling in my hand. "We're here to find a wedding venue for a client."

"A wedding?" Colleen nearly dropped her knife. "You're planning a wedding in Ireland? How exciting." She leaned down the table. "Did you hear that Myrna? They're planning a wedding in Ireland."

"Are the bride and groom Irish?" Myrna asked, and from her expression I knew she thought they should be.

"The bride is," I said, glancing at Richard who was dabbing his piece of bread with butter like TV painter Bob Ross painting happy trees. "I'm not sure about the groom."

"The father of the bride is a senator," Kate added.

The ladies exchanged appreciative nods and whispers, and I shot Kate a look. It wasn't a secret that we were planning the wedding, but I liked to pride Wedding Belles on discretion, so announcing our client to a table of strangers in a pub wasn't my idea of being discreet.

Richard put a hand to his mouth so he could talk behind it. "Don't worry too much, darling. It's not like people know the names of most senators. They aren't real celebrities."

I had to agree with him there. Even though we'd done several weddings for very high-profile politicians, most people wouldn't know their names or be able to recognize them in the street. It was the price to pay for planning weddings in DC and not LA.

The waitress returned to our group and passed out pints of nearly black beer with thick white heads of foam as another young woman took our dinner order. I took my pint and studied it for a moment. I wasn't a huge fan of beer to begin with, although I knew that Ireland's most famous beer was technically a stout. I also knew I couldn't visit the country without drinking at least one.

Myrna stood and patted a hand to her gray hair as she lifted her pint of Guinness. "I'd like to propose a toast on the first night of our trip."

Everyone raised their pints, and Myrna cleared her throat. "To new discoveries."

"To new discoveries," everyone echoed her.

"And new friends," Betty Belle added in her Texas twang, smiling at Richard and me.

Myrna gave a brief nod.

"Slainte," the plump woman next to the tour leader said loudly enough for a few other patrons to turn and raise their glasses.

I noticed Myrna give her a severe look as we all mimicked the Gaelic toast and took drinks. I sipped my Guinness slowly, wiping the foam from my lip when I put it back down. Not bad for beer, I thought. A loud cheer went up from the bar as someone on the television scored a goal of some kind.

"Who was that?" I asked Colleen, nodding to the woman

who had given the toast and whose cheeks were now flushed pink.

"That's Deb from Denver. This isn't her first tour with Myrna."

Betty Belle rolled her eyes. "If you ask me, Myrna uses her like a lackey."

Colleen shifted in her seat. "I don't know. It seems like Deb's one of those people who likes to help."

"She's a hanger-on," Betty Belle said. "She already tracked down all her Irish connections but she still comes and runs around behind Myrna. I think Myrna even covers the cost of the trip for her."

"Now we don't know that," Colleen said.

"It's a well-educated guess." Betty Belle leaned in close. "You can tell she doesn't have money."

Richard nodded along with her, and I knew the Texan was speaking his language. He claimed to be able to spot "new" money at a hundred paces.

"I say if she wants to come on the trip again, why not?" Colleen asked, giving Betty Belle a pointed look. "It's not like you can visit Ireland too many times, right?"

Richard raised his eyebrows at me over his pint. So much for a bunch of sweet grandmas.

"Right," I agreed. "I know we're only scratching the surface while we're here. There are hundreds of castles and manor houses here. We had to narrow it down to the top ones or we'd never be able to leave."

"Where are you off to next?" Colleen asked.

I didn't need to pull out my trip itinerary to remember our stops. It had taken me weeks to research all the best options and then chart our route, so it was burned in my brain. "Dromoland Castle."

"We're going there," Betty Belle said. "At least I think we are. It sounds familiar at least."

"After the Ring of Kerry," Colleen said.

“Here ye are, pet.” The waitress deposited a bowl of Irish stew in front of me.

I watched with amusement as the curvy blonde called Richard “pet,” and his cheeks flushed pink. Richard was not usually one for terms of endearment.

I inhaled the rich aroma of my stew. The widemouthed bowl held big chunks of meat and a brown broth surrounding a fluffy scoop of mashed potatoes. A small plate with more brown bread was placed next to my stew.

Colleen nudged me. "I got the same thing."

I glanced down the table and saw quite a few bowls of stew. Richard had selected a thick steak on a bed of sautéed mushrooms with a metal basket of fries--or chips, as they were called--perched on his plate. As I scooped my first mouthful of stew, I saw Fern jump up and run outside. I caught Kate's eyes, but she just shrugged.

"He probably saw someone wearing an outfit he likes and wants to know where they bought it," Richard said as he cut into his steak. "Don't be surprised if he skips dinner and comes back with shopping bags."

I hadn't seen any high-end clothing boutiques on our way in, but I suspected Richard was right. Less than a minute later, Fern returned with a dazed look on his face.

"Is everything okay?" I asked.

"I thought I saw the cute couple from the plane," he said. "The newlyweds."

"They're here?" I asked before remembering that Fern had given them our entire itinerary.

He shook his head. "When I ran outside I didn't see them. It must have been my imagination."

"That's too bad," Richard said, with not an ounce of sincerity. "I'm sure they'll turn up eventually the way things have been going."

"Richard's right," I said when I noticed that Fern's stunned expression had not changed. "Enjoy your dinner. If they're in

Adare, I'm sure we'll run into them." I dropped my voice. "And I'm sure they'll talk all about their wedding."

"It's not that, Annabelle," Fern said, wringing his hands. "It's the rental car."

My gut tightened. "Please don't tell me we got a parking ticket."

"No." He shook his head slowly. "We didn't get a parking ticket, but you know how Kate didn't quite get the back bumper all the way into the parking space?"

Kate's head snapped up. "Did I hear my name?"

"Well, we don't need to worry about the bumper any more," Fern said. “It's gone. Someone hit the car and crumpled the entire back half of it."

6

"You must be out of your mind," Richard said the next morning when I found him at the top of the double staircase that led into the ballroom's grand foyer. He leaned against the intricate railings that swept down and around the marble stairs underneath the sparkling crystal chandelier.

"Because I asked for a replacement rental car?" I said, taking in the light streaming in the windows and doors leading out to the terrace overlooking the river. "It wasn't our fault that someone came around that corner too fast and plowed into the car and drove off dragging our back bumper."

"Maybe not *our* fault." Richard said as Kate came around the corner, her heels tapping on the floor.

I gave him a warning look. "Do not start this again. Just because she parked a tiny bit over the line doesn't mean the car was fair game. Anyway, she wouldn't have been driving if . . ."

Richard held up his hands. "Fine."

"I'm glad I found you," Kate said, sliding her sunglasses down from where they'd been holding back her hair and taking a sip from her paper cup. "I had to ask a few people to point me in the direction of the new ballroom."

I detected the scent of coffee coming from her cup. "Where did you get that?"

She twitched one shoulder. "You know I have my ways."

I knew her ways often included eyelash batting and showing a little leg, but I wouldn't mind doing a bit of both for a proper cup of coffee.

"Glad you could join us," Richard said. "Fern didn't walk down with you?"

Kate shook her head. "He's stuck on a call with Leatrice." She grinned. "I think he's beginning to regret volunteering to plan her wedding."

"Maybe he's getting a fuller understanding of how hard our job is," I said, feeling more pleased than I'd have liked to admit that Leatrice was torturing him and not me.

"I doubt Leatrice is a typical bride," Kate said.

"Now there's the understatement of the century," Richard said, turning back to me. "What did the rental car company say when you told them about our little mishap?"

"I told them I'd send them the report from the Gardaí showing it wasn't our fault, but they still can't get us a replacement for a couple of days."

"The who-di?" Kate asked.

"The Gardaí," I said. "The Irish police. You know, the guys in uniform who showed up last night."

Kate's eyes brightened. "Those cute boys in blue? I wouldn't mind seeing them again."

"Let's hope that's the last time we need to call them," I said. "And nobody mention our incident to the catering manager we're meeting with. I do not want to be known as the Americans who totaled their rental car within the first twenty-four hours."

Kate put a hand over her mouth as she yawned. "We couldn't get a later appointment? My body thinks it's still nighttime."

"We're supposed to head to Dromoland Castle this afternoon," I said. "Anyway, it's good for us to try to reset our body clocks as quickly as possible."

"How are we supposed to get to Dromoland Castle without a car?" Richard asked, putting his hands on his hips.

"We could always commandeer some sheep to ride," Kate said. "Ireland has lots of sheep."

"Yes," Richard drawled. "Sheep back is definitely the solution."

A petite woman with blond hair walked briskly across the hall with an armful of folders emblazoned with a swirly gold "A." Her black suit was perfectly pressed, and she wore a pearl necklace and matching earrings. I looked down at my white button-down and black pants that still held a few wrinkles from the trip and wished I'd gotten up early enough to iron them.

She extended her hand and smiled widely. "You must be the planners for Hailey Kelly. I'm Sarah." Her Irish accent was soft with just a hint of a singsong lilt.

"I'm Annabelle and this is Kate," I said, taking her hand. "With Wedding Belles. I'm the one you've been speaking with."

"And I'm Richard Gerard." Richard sniffed and held out his hand. "I'm the culinary consultant for the wedding."

Sarah's eyebrows flickered, and I felt reasonably confident she'd never had a client bring in their own culinary consultant before.

"We're delighted the Kellys are considering Adare Manor for their wedding." Sarah began leading us down the stairs. "As you can see, our grand ballroom has a separate entrance which makes it convenient and more private."

We followed her down the stairs and into the foyer, which featured more ivory marble, high French doors, and crystal chandeliers. I held the bannister for balance as I took photos with my phone.

"Guests can enjoy cocktails in the foyer and music from our baby grand piano." She swept a hand to indicate the polished black piano. "Then they proceed into the ballroom for dinner."

She opened one of the doors on one side of the foyer, and we all stepped into the ballroom. I bent my neck to look up at the high ceiling with inset alcoves painted in gold foil that ran down the length of the long room. More glittering chandeliers hung from each alcove, and the room seemed to glow when Sarah turned them on. French doors spanned the length of the far wall, and taupe drapes hung from floor to ceiling, held back with tassels. Instead of the brightly patterned carpet I was accustomed to in hotels, the floor was blond wood in a parquet pattern.

"It's beautiful," I said, taking out my phone and snapping a few more photos for the bride.

Sarah handed us each an Adare Manor folder as we walked back to the foyer. "I've included rate information and sample menus, although we prefer to customize everything for each bride and groom."

Richard opened his folder and began flipping through it. "I'm assuming we can upgrade everything."

Before Sarah could answer, there was a loud tapping at one of the French doors behind us.

Kate lowered her sunglasses. "Is that . . .?"

I felt like slapping a hand over my eyes. "It's Fern." I rushed over to the doors, explaining over my shoulder. "He's our other colleague who was delayed because of a conference call with a client."

I knew it was a stretch to call Leatrice a client or his conversation with her a conference call, but that sounded better than saying our hairstylist friend was gabbing with my nutty neighbor. I unlatched the door and pulled it open.

"I found you," Fern rushed in, breathless. "I've been searching high and low."

"Didn't Kate tell you we'd be in the grand ballroom?" I asked, trying to retain my even-keeled voice.

Fern tapped a finger on his chin and tilted his head. "That sounds vaguely familiar, but I was too distracted by Leatrice. You wouldn't believe what she wants for her wedding."

Before he could launch into what I could only assume would

be a flood of unnecessary details, I cleared my throat. "Fern, this is Sarah. She's the hotel's wedding and event coordinator."

Fern swung his eyes over to her and gave her an appreciative nod as he held out his fingertips. "Did you do that French twist yourself, sweetie? It's divine."

Sarah touched a hand to her hair. "Why, yes."

Fern put a hand on her arm. "It must be so exciting to plan weddings in such a historic manor house."

"I suppose it is," she said, clearly a bit flustered by his compliments and attention.

"Tell me all about the ghosts," Fern said, lowering his voice to a conspiratorial whisper. "A house this old must be haunted."

I tugged Fern away from her. "I'm so sorry. Ignore him."

“Ever since we stayed in a haunted resort, he’s been obsessed,” Kate added.

"What?" Fern said. "The genealogy ladies were talking about ghosts last night at our end of the table."

"Not at Adare Manor I hope," Sarah said with a small gasp.

"Sadly, no." Fern frowned. "They said we'd have better luck at some of the other castles we're visiting."

I narrowed my eyes at him. "What do you mean 'we?'”

"Are you with the other American group?" Sarah asked.

"No," Kate and I both said so forcefully she took a step back.

"Just because we took them up on their offer of a ride back to the hotel last night does not mean we're now part of their group," Richard said, waving a finger at Fern.

"But that's what I came to tell you," Fern bounced up and down on the balls of his feet. "We don't need to worry about getting a new rental car or about Richard driving us around and almost running off the road."

Richard opened his mouth and let out a small sound of indignant protest.

"The ladies have officially invited us to join them in their minibus," Fern said. "Isn't that wonderful? They said there's plenty of room, and they even agreed to adjust to our timeline.

Apparently we were heading to most of the same spots anyway, so it only means adding a night at Dromoland for them. As long as we're okay with a few extra tea and bathroom breaks." He gave me a look. "Not everyone can be a camel like you, Annabelle."

"You must be insane if you think I'm going to spend the next week riding around in a tour bus," Richard said.

"It's not technically a tour bus," Fern said. "It's a private charter and you know it only seats fifteen. It's not like I'm suggesting we hop on a Greyhound."

Richard put the back of his hand to his forehead. "I'm feeling a bit faint."

I put a hand under his elbow, knowing what the mention of public transportation usually did to him. I glanced at Sarah. “I’m so sorry. You were telling us about upgrades.”

The woman looked a bit stunned as Richard fanned himself. “We can certainly offer upgrades for your client.”

“You know, this does solve our problem," Kate said.

I bit the edge of my bottom lip, knowing she was right. I wasn't crazy about being cooped up in a van with virtual strangers, but I also knew we only had a few days to knock out all the venues on our list. Our client would not care about excuses, even very good ones.

"And you rejected my suggestion about going on sheep back," Kate said with a grin.

Fern looked from me to Kate. "Is that really a thing?"

Sarah's head ping-ponged between us as she tried to follow the conversation, and her mouth had dropped open at the mention of sheep-back travel.

Richard fanned his face with both hands. "A minibus? You know I don't do mini anything. No mini malls, no mini fridges, no minibuses." He dropped his voice. "I don't even do MINI-Coopers."

"Do you want to explain to Senator Kelly why we had to eliminate venues from his daughter's list?" I asked Richard.

He glared at me before throwing his hands into the air. "Fine. We'll share the bus with the old ladies."

"One thing." Fern held up a finger. "You can't call them 'old ladies.' The correct term is 'chronologically enhanced.'"

"Heaven preserve us," Richard said, looking up at the ceiling.

"Over here we like to say two people shorten the road," Sarah said in an obvious attempt to be helpful.

Fern clapped his hands. "This is going to be so much fun."

Kate turned to Sarah and me. "I feel like the saying might not apply to *those* two people."

7

I stumbled down the short flight of stairs from the minibus to the pavement, grateful to be at Dromoland Castle. Even though the trip from Adare Manor should have taken less than an hour, we'd gotten bogged down in traffic through the city of Limerick, and then we'd stopped at Bunratty Castle as a combination bathroom break and cultural stop. What I'd assumed would be a short stop to peer up at the medieval castle had morphed into a full exploration of the recreated nineteenth century Irish village nearby. I'd eventually had to drag Fern from the gift shop before he could buy up every last tea towel in stock.

"Now this looks like a castle," Kate said, stepping down next to me and running a hand through her hair.

The gray stone castle featured both round and square turrets soaring up from the corners of the building. A lake sat to one side, and a long curving drive led to the front door of the castle. Like at Adare Manor, ivy crawled up some of the castellated walls.

"Every building looks like a castle in Ireland." Richard stomped off of the bus behind us, his eyes flicking up to the impressive structure. "I feel like I've seen enough castles in the past two days to do me for a lifetime."

"We just got here," Kate said, "and we've only been to two venues. We'll barely scratch the surface of castles here."

"Don't remind me." Richard hiked his duffel bag high on his shoulder.

I stared at the blue velour hoodie draped around his shoulders. "This time I get to ask. What are you wearing?"

Richard cut his eyes to himself. "One of the ladies I insisted I wear this when I got cold. It may be hideous, but it's actually quite warm."

"Hideous things usually are," Kate muttered.

Richard shot Kate a look and pulled off the hoodie. "It's bad enough I had to listen to show tunes the entire way, but if we're going to stop at every castle in the country with a gift shop, we're never going to make it back to DC."

"It wasn't the singing that got to me," I said, rubbing my head. "It was the perfume. Every one of those ladies is wearing a different scent."

"And the redheaded hippie is wearing patchouli," Richard said, crinkling his nose to let me know exactly what he thought of that.

"You can't beat the fresh air in the Irish countryside," Kate said as she took a deep breath of the cool air. "I wouldn't mind living here. Maybe we should consider a Wedding Belles branch in Ireland, Annabelle."

"First things first," I said. "We have to prove we can successfully plan a wedding here before we open up an office."

Kate flapped a hand at me. "Details, details. Just think of it, Annabelle. A market where no one knows about all the unfortunate incidents at our weddings."

By "unfortunate incidents" I knew Kate meant the number of dead bodies that had happened to turn up at our weddings over the years. Luckily there were still plenty of brides in DC who'd never heard we'd become experts in wedding day crime solving, but I couldn't deny that the murders hadn't been great for business.

"Except for all the people in the minibus," Richard said, giving her a stern look. "You and Fern told them everything."

"Not everything," Kate said. "Just the highlights. Anyway, these ladies don't live in Ireland. They're spread all over the U.S. It's not like we want to start planning weddings in Iowa or South Dakota."

"The driver is from Ireland," Richard said. "You didn't notice Seamus's shocked expression when you talked about finding the body impaled on the ice sculpture?"

Kate shifted from one high-heeled boot to the other. "No, I didn't know he was listening."

Richard narrowed his eyes at her. "The bus only holds fifteen people, Kate. I've been in larger bathrooms. Of course he heard every word. I just hope he doesn't think we're dangerous Americans bringing crime with us."

"Who, us?" Kate said. "Who could ever think we're dangerous?"

Fern came down off the bus, his arms laden with shopping bags. "Did you hear they have archery here? I can't wait to learn to shoot like Robin Hood."

"Now that's deadly. Keep me far away from Fern with a bow and arrow," said Richard, with a furtive glance toward the disembarking retirees. "If you don't mind, I'm going to run inside and get our room keys before Myrna beats me to it."

Richard hurried toward the entrance, his Gucci bag bouncing behind him.

I took a deep breath, inhaling the fresh scent of cut grass and flowers. We must not be far from the walled gardens I'd read about. I hoped they would be the perfect location for our bride's wedding ceremony, and I couldn't wait to see them. I felt my phone vibrate in my bag and pulled it out, glancing at the name on the screen and letting out a small groan.

Kate looked over my shoulder. "At least it isn't a bride. I

mean, a bride who's hired us."

"Hi, Leatrice," I said when I answered. "Everything okay in the building?"

I heard a deep sigh on the other end. "The building is fine, dear. I still think the new couple from the second floor seem suspicious. He says he works for the Treasury Department, but you know what that means."

Probably that he worked for the Treasury Department, I thought, but didn't say anything. Leatrice saw a conspiracy theory around every corner and had been known to run her own surveillance ops on various neighbors.

"How is Hermès?" I asked, hearing a faint yip in the background.

"Oh, we're having a grand old time," Leatrice said. "You know how he loves watching old movies."

I knew how much Leatrice loved watching old movies, and I suspected Richard's Yorkie loved napping next to her while she did so.

"It's not Hermès that's the problem," Leatrice said.

"There's a problem?" I took a few steps away from Fern and Kate as the rest of the ladies spilled out of the bus.

"I don't like to complain." Another long breath. "But Fern is driving me crazy."

"What?" I wasn't used to people driving Leatrice crazy. Usually it was the other way around.

"You know I adore him," Leatrice said, her words coming out in a rush. "It's the wedding planning. He's going a bit overboard, and I don't know how to rein him in."

"What do you mean by overboard?" I'd had clients want everything from cakes shaped like squirrels to gnomes as a reception decor, so there wasn't much that could surprise me.

"I didn't mind the idea of Hermès being the ring bearer," Leatrice said. "Or of him wearing a tiny tuxedo. But I'm not sure if murder should be the theme of the wedding."

"Fern wants you to have a murder-themed wedding?" I

glanced behind me to where my hairstylist friend was giggling and laughing with a pair of white-haired ladies.

"He said that since I've been involved in so many of the investigations during your weddings, we could design a wedding around it. Like those murder mystery theaters where one of the guests dies during the evening."

"You're going to kill off one of your wedding guests?" Nothing screamed romance like homicide.

"Fern thinks it would be fun to have the rest of the guests solve the murder," Leatrice said. "Unfortunately, he wants my sweetie pie to be the one murdered."

I took another peek at Fern who was pawing through his shopping bags and showing the ladies his castle tea towels. "So let me get this straight. Fern wants to pretend that Sidney Allen--the groom at your wedding--has been murdered and make everyone solve his murder during the reception? Is your fiancé supposed to lie on the floor and pretend to be dead at his own wedding?"

"That's exactly what he asked," Leatrice said with a giggle. "I've always thought you and my love muffin are simpatico, Annabelle."

I suspected it was less about me being in tune with her love muffin and more about both of us being rational.

"Don't worry," I said. "I'll talk to Fern. You don't have to have a murder-themed wedding if you don't want to. Actually, I'd recommend you don't. I think we've all had enough murder at weddings for one lifetime."

I heard Leatrice let out her breath with a long whoosh. "I knew you'd know what to do, dearie."

"What kind of wedding do you want to have?" I asked. "And keep in mind you don't need to have a theme."

"I was thinking of keeping it simple," Leatrice said. "Something small with just the people closest to us. You and Reese, Kate, Richard, Fern, Buster, and Mac. And of course baby Merry and Prue."

I swallowed a lump that had formed in my throat. The friends she'd named were all my friends. "Does Sydney Allen have any family or friends he wants to invite?"

"No family. At least none he's close to. He might invite some of his best performers. And maybe a few of the caterers who have referred him the most over the years."

The lump in my throat grew as I realized that Sydney Allen's friends and family consisted of a few work acquaintances and employees. It made me even happier that he and Leatrice had found each other. And it made me determined that their wedding was not going to be some crazy disaster.

I looked back at Fern and Kate as they grabbed their luggage from the pile being unloaded from the minibus, and I noticed Kate pulling my small, wheeled suitcase along with her own. Fern snagged his Louis Vuitton duffel, and I saw with some surprise that it wasn't the only bag in the pile with the signature interlocking "L" and "V." He'd been right about the ladies. They were more well-heeled than their sweatsuits would indicate.

"Kate and I will talk to Fern, and then we'll come up with something small and simple that's perfect for you two," I said.

"I knew I could count on you to fix things," Leatrice said.

I noticed Richard hurrying back out of the castle. "I've got to run, but don't worry. I've got everything handled."

I hung up as Richard reached me.

"I got all our keys," he said, flipping through four paper folders. "Now I don't know about you, but I'm going up to my room and not coming out for hours."

I took one of the keys. A few hours of solitude sounded perfect. Then I looked at the time on my phone and frowned. "We have a meeting with the events manager in two hours, and I was hoping to get some photos of the grounds before then. How does a one-hour break sound?"

Richard huffed out a breath. "It sounds like barely enough time for an outfit refresh, but I suppose I'll survive."

"You don't need to change," I told him. "It's just a tour."

He wrinkled his nose. "This outfit has dust from a recreated Irish village on it. I'd like to make a good impression on the events manager, thank you very much." He flicked his eyes down my jeans and sweater. "I trust you're being ironic with those jeans, darling."

I'd never once in my life considered being ironic with my clothing, but I nodded. "Obviously."

"Good." He spun on his heel. "I'll see you in an hour."

Colleen rushed up to me, her bright-green fanny pack jiggling around her waist, and grabbed my arm. "Was it all true?"

I looked at her wide eyes and wondered if she'd snuck in a pint or two at our stop in Bunratty Castle. I did remember there being a pub in the attached village. "Was what true?"

"All the stories about the cases you solved for the police during your weddings?"

I cringed even though Reese couldn't hear, because I knew what he'd say about Kate claiming we'd solved the cases for him. "I wouldn't exactly phrase it like that, but we have gotten sucked into a few investigations."

She looked over her shoulder. "I can't talk now, but I'd love to ask you about something later."

"Okay." The last thing I wanted was to spend the entire trip talking about our weddings gone wrong. Weddings seemed to be a subject that everyone loved to talk about, and when you added murder to that, no one could get enough. I took a step closer to Colleen as the driver unloaded more bags onto the pile behind me. "I'm popping up to my room to change, but I'll be back down in an hour to walk around the grounds if that works for you. We need to check out the walled garden as a possible ceremony venue."

She squeezed my hand. "Perfect. I guess it's my good fortune we ended up on the same bus."

I tried to smile. I had not wanted to spend the trip discussing the deadly side of my job. I followed Kate and Fern into the castle. I'd have to have a serious chat with both of them later.

8

"Finally," Richard said, picking up his pace as we approached the black door within the stone wall. "I knew we'd find it even though the directions we were given were abysmal."

We'd walked from the castle along the lake until we'd located the gate leading into the famous walled garden. Since this was one of the potential spots for a ceremony, I wanted to take plenty of photos to send back to our bride. I read the sign to the right of the door that read "Walled Garden" then the ones affixed to the door asking visitors to close the gate behind them and to be advised of the deep pond in the garden. Ivy and tiny purple flowers climbed up the crumbling stone and made it easy to believe the garden was two hundred years old.

"It's certainly authentic," Kate said, touching a hand to the stone.

Fern tossed a new scarf over one shoulder—ivory fabric with green Celtic symbols entwined along the border that he'd fastened with a silver Celtic brooch--another purchase from Bunratty village, I assumed. "It would make for a dramatic procession."

Richard opened the door and we entered the garden. I

inhaled the sweet scent of flowers. Even though it was only April, the beds were blooming with colorful blossoms and the lawn was green. I took out my phone and snapped a few photos.

"Didn't you say one of the ladies was supposed to join us?" Fern asked, striding forward.

"She might have changed her mind," I said. We'd waited for her for an extra ten minutes before leaving the lobby, so I didn't feel guilty for going on without Colleen. "That reminds me." I shot a look at both Kate and Fern. "No more talking about the murders at our weddings."

"Why not?" Fern asked. "Everyone loves hearing about it, especially my heroic part in the stories."

I saw Richard raise an eyebrow as I continued. "I do not want people in Ireland to know our reputation. If we do end up doing more weddings here, I'd prefer not to be known as the wedding planners of death."

Fern made a face. "Fine, but I always thought that nickname gave you an air of mystery."

I glared at him. "Did you give us that nickname?" Fern loved nothing more than sharing juicy gossip or giving a creative moniker.

His cheeks colored and he focused intently on the bushes by the entrance. "I only ever said you were deadly efficient."

I wasn't sure I believed him, but I let it go. Following the path over a short stone bridge, we walked above the long rectangular pond filled with lily pads. My eyes were drawn to the flowering bushes that lined the path past the water as I imagined our bride walking between them in her wedding gown. "This could work," I said.

Fern strode ahead. "But it's not very Irish, is it?" He waved a hand. "I mean, there's a palm tree for goodness sake."

"Ireland has a very temperate climate," Richard said, reading from his guidebook as he eyed the tall tree that looked better suited to a beach than a walled garden.

"We just came from a castle with turrets," I said. "I don't

think anyone will forget we're in Ireland just by seeing one palm tree."

Fern shrugged. "We could always add some elements to make it more Irish."

"Like what?" I put one hand on my hip. "Leprechauns instead of bridesmaids?"

Fern beamed at me. "Great idea, Annabelle. I knew you'd get on board eventually." He swirled his hands over his head as he walked forward. "The flower girls could toss shamrocks instead of flower petals. It would be adorable."

"Maybe we could teach the bridal party one of those Riverdances," Kate said. "You know how Indian weddings do Bollywood dances?"

I shook my head. "I was joking about the leprechauns. No way am I putting my name on a wedding with a Riverdancing bridal party. All the bridesmaids and groomsmen are American. It would be like a flurry of left feet."

Fern frowned. "You've never been open to theme weddings."

"Speaking of that," I said, seeing my opening and deciding to go for it, "I'm not sure if a murder-themed wedding is the best choice for Leatrice."

He spun his head around and his man bun bobbled on top of his head. "How did you know . . .? Oh, I see. She told you my ideas, didn't she?"

"That you wanted to have the groom pretend to be dead for most of the reception?" I asked. "Yes, she mentioned it."

"You want an elderly groom to play dead during his own wedding?" Kate asked. "Don't you think that's a little on the nose?"

I swatted at Kate. "They aren't *that* old."

Actually, I knew Leatrice was over eighty, even if I wasn't completely sure how far along Sidney Allen was in his seventies. Still, I didn't like to think of Leatrice getting up there in years. She'd been one of the steadiest parts of my life since I'd moved to DC, even if she did drive me a little bit crazy. And after a recent scare, I did not want to be reminded of her mortality.

"What ever happened to a classic wedding?" Richard asked, his voice raised. "White flowers, a white dress, a tiered wedding cake, and champagne served at the reception. Now every wedding has to push the envelope. Pink wedding dresses, bridal bouquets made entirely out of succulents, wedding cakes that are actually Rice Krispy treats, signature drinks named after the couple's dog. Would everyone please stop trying to be unique and just have some taste?"

He stomped off down the path leaving us all staring at each other.

"Do you think it was the dead groom or the leprechauns that pushed him over the edge?" Fern asked after a moment.

"I don't know, but neither helped," I said.

"He's been a little high-strung since we got here, don't you think?" Kate asked.

Fern trilled two fingers against his chin. "More than usual you mean?"

"I'll go talk to him," I said. "You two figure out the best place for a ceremony." I held up a finger. "A ceremony that does not include anything goofy."

I could hear Fern grumbling as I walked away, but I focused on catching up to Richard who was already at the second set of stone steps leading up to a higher level of the garden.

"So, was that just the jet lag talking, or is something really bothering you?" I asked when I reached him at the top of the third stone step.

He let out a breath. "You mean aside from the driving debacle, followed by the even more catastrophic carpooling incident, topped off by the insanity of our colleagues?"

"Yes," I said. "Aside from that."

He pursed his lips and looked away, then glanced back at me. "Fine. It's more than that. I called in to the office when I went up to my room. We've had no new inquiries since I've been away."

"But we've only been here two days," I said. "Plus, it's April. Not exactly the busiest booking month."

"Maybe not for weddings, but I usually book a lot of corporate work in the spring." He didn't meet my eyes. "I'm afraid the latest scandals have scared off my business for good."

Richard had been convinced a recent and unfair murder accusation would tank his catering business, and I'd been just as convinced that it would all blow over.

"We have a bunch of weddings together on the books, including this one, which is about as high-profile as you can get in DC," I reminded him. "How many caterers are spending the week in Ireland?"

He gave me a weak smile. "True. Your clients have been the only things keeping me in the black. But you won't be able to force every couple to use me. It isn't good for your business."

"Don't worry about my business." I put a hand on his sleeve. "You sent me leads when I was first starting out and didn't know anybody."

"Anybody?" Richard said. "You didn't know any *thing*, darling. You were as green as they come."

"Fine." I arched an eyebrow at him. "You still hired me. I'm just returning the favor. It's not like you aren't the best in the city."

Richard gave a sniff. "Also true. I just hope this wedding will put me back in the spotlight."

I linked my arm through his. "If a million-dollar destination wedding for a senator's daughter who's marrying a Silicon Valley genius doesn't do it, I don't know what will."

"I hope you're right. I'm too old for a 'side hustle.'" He made air quotes. "If I have to resort to selling face cream door-to-door, promise me you'll put me out of my misery."

"I'm pretty sure the face creams are sold over Facebook these days."

He put a hand to his forehead. "Even worse."

Fern bustled up to us, separated our arms by inserting himself between us, and propelled us forward by the elbows. "Kate and I have had a brilliant idea about the ceremony. And before you ask, there are no dancers or green top hats involved."

"Thank you," I said. "I know that was a sacrifice."

"You have no idea." He stopped us at the foot of the bridge. "Since you want classic but none of us want boring, Kate thought we could flip it around for the processional."

"I hope you don't mean have people walk backward," I said.

He shook his head. "Instead of walking in from the stone gate, we have the stone gate be the ceremony backdrop."

I stared at the tall stone arch flanked by two ball topiaries with greenery-covered stone walls extending in both directions. "That's not a bad idea. It's pretty the way it is, but if we did some floral decor it could be stunning."

"You like?" Kate asked from the middle of the bridge. "We thought we'd have the bridal party be staggered on the steps of the bridge and the bride and groom in the middle."

I left Fern and Richard to join her. "It's the highest point so all the guests could see them." I scanned the gardens from my vantage point then twisted to face the arched entrance. "But the gate is still high enough to see over. You know, it just might work."

"There's more." Kate rubbed her hands together. "I thought we could fill the water below with flowers in the bride's colors."

"Unless she likes the look of lily pads better," I said, stepping to the side and looking over at the water. My eye caught on something bright green peeking out from under the bridge. I blinked a few times as I realized it wasn't a natural shade of green. I clutched the stone wall and leaned over to get a better look as my heart began to hammer in my chest. I jerked back up and stumbled off the bridge, pressing my hand to my mouth.

"What?" Kate gaped at me and ran to the side of the bridge to look over. "Is that . . .?"

"Is there something in the moat?" Fern asked as he joined Kate on the bridge.

"It's not a moat," Richard said. "It's not technically around the castle."

"Moat, pond, whatever," Fern said, peering down and sucking in air. "There's a body down there." He looked up and met my eyes, his own round with surprise. "That lady you were talking to at dinner. The one with the fanny pack."

I looked away so I wouldn't have to get another glimpse of the wet gray hair fanned around her head as Colleen floated face up in the water. Dead.

9

"I can't believe it." Betty Belle sat on a low upholstered chair in the lobby of Dromoland Castle as Fern patted her hand. "She said she wanted to go see the gardens, but I never expected . . ."

"There, there." Fern produced a handkerchief with a flourish and handed it to the sniffling woman. "You couldn't have known."

After we'd reported finding Colleen's body floating in the long garden pond--with Fern running ahead shrieking the whole way back to the castle--we'd been waiting with the genealogy tour group in the lobby. The local Gardaí had arrived and reported directly to the walled garden, while the hotel staff had been doing their best to keep us corralled and calm, not an easy task since we were spread out across the hotel's entrance.

I glanced over at Myrna, the steel-haired leader of the tour group, as she stood next to one of the standing suits of armor flanking an ornately carved wooden desk. An arrangement of white lilies topped the desk, and even from a few yards away, I could smell their sweet scent. Myrna's lips were set in a hard line as she spoke to one of the hotel employees, and she appeared to be giving the suits of armor a run for their money when it came to being intimidating. Deb, the woman Betty Belle had deemed a "lackey," hovered near Myrna holding two cups of tea.

Even though heavy drapes hung at the windows and tapestries covered the walls, the gray stone walls along one side of the long lobby made the space feel cold. Crystal chandeliers hung from the wood crossbeamed ceiling and lightened up the maroon carpeting and matching walls, but it still felt very much like the castle it was. I rubbed my arms to warm up from the chill I hadn't been able to shake since seeing Colleen floating in the water.

"How are you holding up, hon?" Nancy asked, patting Betty Belle on the shoulder.

Betty Belle blew her nose into Fern's handkerchief. "Aside from my roommate being found dead you mean?" She gave a small shake of her head. "I'm sorry. That was rude of me."

The redhead smiled at her. "Don't even think twice about it. I know you and Colleen hit it off when you finally met in person. It's a shock for all of us."

"You were roommates?" I asked Betty Belle.

She nodded, dabbing at her eyes. "We got to know each other through the Facebook group and ended up messaging each other and swapping recipes. Colleen was the one who convinced me to come on the trip. It made sense for us to room together." Her voice broke. "We thought it would be fun."

Richard walked up and jerked his head to one side, indicating I should join him. I gave Betty Belle's leg a final pat as I surrendered my seat to Nancy and joined Richard next to the tufted leather couch by the front door.

He handed me a teacup edged with delicate flowers. "This will help you warm up, darling. You look like you're freezing."

I gratefully wrapped my hands around the warmth of the cup and took a sip of the hot tea. "Thank you. Where did you get it?"

He flicked his eyes behind me. "I might have poached it

from afternoon tea. If we have to wait any longer, I'm going back for tea sandwiches and pastries."

"How much longer do you think we'll be here?" I asked, scanning the ladies clustered on chairs and love seats, all in various stages of weeping.

"Not long, I hope. It can't be good for business to have all this sobbing in the lobby."

I narrowed my eyes at him. "Be nice. They've just lost their friend. I'm sure the police will question us soon and then release us."

"Gardaí," Richard corrected me. "The Irish call their police the Gardaí, remember? And I'm not sure it will be the friendly experience we're used to with law enforcement since none of us are dating an officer."

"Give it time," I said as I spotted Kate walking through the main doors beside a tall man in a dark-blue uniform. His hair was light brown and he had a square jaw with either a well-trimmed beard or several days of stubble. Even though I had a boyfriend, I couldn't help looking twice at him.

"So much for this going quickly," Richard mumbled. "We'll be lucky if Kate agrees to leave the country with us."

I started to tell him he was being silly, but I saw the way she looked at the man and thought better of it. I caught her eye and waved her over.

"Where have you been?" I asked when she stepped away from the garda.

She let out a breathy sigh. "Just giving a statement to Connor Ryan."

"You're on a first-name basis?" Richard shook his head. "What kind of statement did you give him? A profession of your love and devotion or perhaps your room number?"

Kate jabbed him with her elbow. "I'll have you know he's been perfectly professional." She frowned. "It's a bit frustrating."

"I can imagine," Richard said. "I don't suppose you learned

anything about the poor dead woman in the midst of all the eyelash batting?"

Before Kate could answer, the good-looking garda approached us, extending a hand and making eye contact. "Garda Ryan. You two also found the body, eh?"

Richard and I both shook his hand, and I felt myself blush as he held my gaze with his very blue eyes. I heard Richard clear his throat and looked over to see his cheeks also flushed. The garda didn't seem to notice his effect as he took out a notebook and flipped it open.

The familiar action made me think about Reese. A part of me wished he was here and another part was glad he wasn't witnessing us being involved in yet another investigation. My only consolation was that no one in the DC wedding industry would hear about this. It wasn't good for business to have such a high body count at our weddings, and I'd as soon keep this latest one--although technically not associated with one of our weddings--quiet.

The garda shifted his eyes to me. "Your business partner has given me a rundown of the timeline, but I'd like you to tell me in your own words."

My head snapped to Kate when he mentioned "business partner," but I didn't comment on it. She was too enamored with the cute officer to notice my surprise anyway.

"There's not much to tell," I said. "We were walking in the walled garden. We'd only been there a few minutes."

"Can't you get all this from the security cameras?" Richard asked.

"There are no cameras in the gardens," Garda Ryan said, then turned his attention back to me. "Did you see anyone else in the garden when you arrived?"

I thought for a moment. "Not that I remember. No one in view at least."

"And you didn't see the deceased immediately?"

I shook my head. "We walked over the bridge without

looking down." I looked at Richard. "My friend and I walked ahead a bit, to the short flight of stone steps at the end of the path, then our other friend Fern came to get us and we walked back to the bridge. It was only when I went to the middle of the bridge and looked over that I saw her. Actually, it was her green fanny pack that caught my eye."

Garda Ryan jotted a few words in his notebook before looking up. "You didn't touch the body?"

I shivered and shook my head. "We didn't get closer than looking over the bridge. It was obvious even from there that she was dead."

"How so?" he asked.

I rubbed my arms again as I recalled the look of open-mouthed shock on the dead woman's face. "Her eyes were wide, and her skin already looked blue."

"This isn't our first dead body, Garda Ryan," Kate said.

He stared at the three of us while I groaned inwardly. So much for us keeping our past involvements in investigations under wraps. "You don't say?"

"We've had a few incidents at our weddings," I said, trying to sound as nonchalant as possible. "Nothing that has to do with this though."

He wrote more in his notebook. "Did you recognize her right away?"

I tried to push the image of her wide unblinking eyes out of my mind. "Yes. We'd met yesterday and had dinner together, so I knew who she was."

"Yesterday was the first time you'd met her?" His eyes moved from me to Richard.

"We might have arrived in the same bus, but we're not with their group," Richard said. "We just happened to meet yesterday when we were all at Adare Manor."

The garda angled his head. "And you decided to share a van?"

"It's a bit more complicated that that," I said. "We had a rental car, but it was involved in an accident."

He nodded his head as if that explained everything. "We have quite a few accidents involving American tourists each year."

Richard drew himself up to his full height. "I'll have you know that this American did not get in an accident. We were hit by another car while we were parked."

"Our car might have been sticking out into the street," I admitted.

Kate crossed her arms and gave me a look. "Are you suggesting that my parking was the reason some maniac crashed into us?"

Garda Ryan raised an eyebrow, and I felt like I'd seen the same look of amusement on Reese's face before.

"That's how we ended up sharing a ride with the genealogy tour group," I said, giving both Kate and Richard a warning look. "They were heading to Dromoland and so were we, and they were kind enough to offer us a ride."

"So you three aren't here on a genealogy trip?"

Kate touched a hand to his arm. "We're wedding planners. We're here to find the perfect venue for a wedding." She smiled up at him. "Not mine, of course."

Richard groaned while the garda nodded and made another note in his pad.

"The gentleman with the ponytail is also with us." I pointed to Fern, who still sat next to Betty Belle. It appeared that he'd moved from comforting her to touching up her makeup.

"So you didn't know any of the other women before yesterday even though you're all Americans?"

"No," I told him. "We're from DC and they came from all over the country."

Kate leaned into him. "It's a big country, you know."

Another garda--this one a petite woman with blond hair tucked up under her hat--stepped inside and walked over to us. Her eyes dropped to Kate's hand on her colleague's arm and then to him. "You need help with the questioning?"

He gave a curt shake of his head. "Almost done here. Why don't you start with the ladies over there?"

"The one with the white hair was her roommate," I said. "Her name is Betty Belle."

Garda Ryan nodded his head at me. "That's helpful. She might have a better idea who would want to harm the victim."

The female officer headed for Betty Belle, and Garda Ryan flipped his notebook closed.

"Wait a second," I said. "Did you say who would want to harm the victim?"

Richard put a hand over his eyes and groaned. "Please say it isn't so."

"This wasn't an accident?" I asked, trying to keep my voice down as I saw Fern look over. "We assumed Colleen slipped and fell into the pond."

Kate dropped her hand from the officer's arm. "She didn't hit her head on a rock and drown?"

His handsome face twisted for a moment. "I suppose you'll know soon enough that this is a homicide investigation. You probably couldn't see from above, but the victim had ligature marks on her neck."

Richard raised a hand to his own throat. "So she was . . .?"

"Strangled?" Fern cried, stepping from behind the garda, his word piercing the quiet of the lobby and making everyone gasp.

10

"So much for keeping the fact that Colleen was murdered a secret," I said as I flopped faceup across the king-size bed. Even though it was already early evening, light poured in from the window overlooking the lake. It felt odd to have the sun setting at almost nine o'clock at night, although I'd heard it would set even later during the summer months.

Richard perched on the upholstered bench at the end of the bed. "Discretion is not in Fern's wheelhouse."

"True." Fern's stylish Georgetown hair salon was known as the place to go for precision haircuts and juicy gossip. Some of it Fern acquired from his high-profile clients and some he made up himself. If you wanted a secret kept, you did not tell Fern.

Since I'd done little more than drop off my suitcase when we'd first arrived, I rolled over on the bed and took in the room. Unlike Adare Manor, the rooms at Dromoland had a distinctly modern design with the four poster bed made out of an ash-colored wood and topped with unadorned round finials. Soft gray drapes hung at the window, and a gray-and-white-plaid carpet covered the floor. A gray velour love seat held mustard-yellow throw pillows while a pair of matching armless chairs sat in a raised alcove that housed another window.

"I can't believe we didn't catch that." I let my cheek sink back onto the soft duvet.

"Catch what?"

I didn't lift my head. "The marks on her neck. We've seen enough dead bodies to notice something like that. Unless they were so fresh when we found her that they hadn't become bruises yet."

Richard shuddered. "Living with a detective has made you quite gruesome, darling. Anyway, we didn't get close enough to spot bruises, and if I remember correctly, the old dear had on a mock turtleneck."

"Good eyes. I'd forgotten that." I raised myself onto one elbow.

"I only remember because I thought to myself that I hadn't seen one of those since the '90s." He shook his head. "I only hope when I go that I'm better dressed."

"If I find you dead in a mock turtleneck, I'll know there was foul play involved," I said.

"Indeed you will. If you find me in anything off the rack, I expect you to demand a full investigation."

I grinned, despite the macabre topic, and rolled over to stare up at the smooth white ceiling. "So either the marks were hidden or they were new."

"Or both. She couldn't have been out there too long," Richard said, crossing his legs at the knee and pumping one foot up and down. "If I remember correctly, you barely gave us time to breathe before dragging us out to walk the property."

"I wanted to scout out the garden while there was good light," I said as I thought back to the timing of the afternoon. "Colleen must have gone straight to the garden to have made it there in enough time to get strangled and dumped into the pond before we arrived."

Richard stopped bobbing his foot and stood up. "Oh no. I know what's happening here."

"What?" I rolled my head over to watch as his foot bobbing became foot tapping, the pace equally impatient.

Richard leveled a finger at me. "Might I remind you we're here to scout out wedding venues, not get embroiled in another murder investigation?"

"You don't think I wanted us to find a body, do you? It's not like I planned this, Richard, but like it or not, we are involved."

He threw his arms in the air. "This is like that law of attraction stuff. You're a murder magnet."

I thought those were bold words considering he'd recently been suspect number one in a murder investigation. "This is nothing more than a coincidence."

"You think it's a coincidence that a perfectly normal old lady gets knocked off the day after she meets us?" Richard asked, his voice more high-pitched than usual.

"How could we have anything to do with it?" I argued. "We only met the tour group yesterday, and it was only by chance we ended up riding with them."

"Was it though?" Richard paced a small circle at the foot of the bed. "What if this was all a setup to get us to find her? Wasn't she supposed to go on the walk with us?"

"Yes," I admitted, "but that might have been a coincidence. Colleen was the one who wanted to talk with me, so I invited her to join our walk. I hardly think she'd set us up for her own murder. Why would anyone want to set us up anyway?"

He stopped short. "Well, if I knew that then I'd probably know who was behind it, wouldn't I?"

"I think you're getting worked up over nothing," I said. "Aside from finding the body, we have nothing to do with it. We barely knew her, and we certainly don't know why anyone would want to strangle her. I promise you, I have no intention of getting sucked into another murder case." I sat up. "As a matter of fact, I should probably take photos of the rooms before we mess them up too much. Our bride will want photos of the rooms her guests would be staying in."

"We just discovered a dead body outside a castle," Richard said. "How can you think about work?"

"I thought you didn't want to get embroiled in the murder case." I scooted to the edge of the bed. "So let's focus on the wedding. As sad as I am about Colleen, you know our bride won't consider a murder any reason for us not to do our job."

"Isn't that the truth?" Richard grumbled. "Maybe if one of us had died it would be a different story."

"Maybe," I said. "And that's a big maybe."

Richard looked at me, the corner of his mouth twitching up into a grin. "Can you think of any reason a bride would find compelling enough to put her wedding on the back burner?"

I tapped my chin. "Aside from World War III, nothing springs to mind. We've had category four hurricanes, code orange terror levels, and dead bodies not stop them."

"We really should get hazard pay." Richard started laughing, and I joined him. Somehow laughing about our clients' crazy demands felt therapeutic.

"At least we're in it together," I said, once again feeling grateful for my team and for the fact that I hadn't been alone when I'd spied Colleen floating in the water.

"Is that another way of saying misery loves company?" Richard winked at me, crossed to the desk, and flipped open a leather folder. "I don't think I can bear going down to the dining room tonight. How do you feel about ordering room service?"

I let out a breath. "That sounds perfect. I know the genealogy tour group was scheduled to eat in the fancy restaurant. Do you think they'll cancel?"

Richard shrugged. "Myrna doesn't seem like the type to change her plans, but I can't imagine that would be a fun meal."

I hopped off the bed and crossed to the desk, leaning over Richard to read the menu. "Chocolate and Bailey's mousse. Double yum."

"That's dessert, darling. You can't just get dessert."

"Well, I don't think I can stomach anything heavy." I ran my finger down the list of entrees then flipped back one page. "Maybe a bowl of the Atlantic Way seafood chowder. And the mousse."

"The sirloin in red wine jus looks delicious."

"Didn't you have steak last night?" I asked. "Are you planning on eating anything traditionally Irish while we're here?"

Richard hooked a hand on his hip. "You mean like potatoes? The steak comes with chips."

I gave him what I hoped was a withering look. "Steak and fries is not Irish. What about the lamb stew or bangers and mash?"

He looked down his nose at me. "Do I really strike you as a 'bangers and mash' person?" He gave a brusque shake of his head. "I do not like my food to have that many verbs."

I blew out a breath. "Fine." I dug my phone out of my purse. "I'm going to text Kate and Fern and tell them we're staying in for dinner."

"Knowing how close Fern is with the old ladies, he's probably sitting at the head of their table or planning Colleen's wake."

I shuddered to think what kind of wake Fern would come up with. "Let's hope for Colleen's sake, he's not." I fired off a pair of texts then took a few quick shots of the room, pulling my rolling suitcase out of the way and smoothing the white duvet where I'd been lying.

I glanced down at the text that popped up on my phone. "Kate's on her way and she wants us to order her the Irish salmon. No word from Fern."

"I told you," Richard muttered. "He's jumped ship and is with the sweatpants brigade."

"Be nice. I've been known to wear sweats."

He gave me a look that told me exactly what he thought of my wardrobe choices. "You know Karl Lagerfeld said that wearing sweatpants was giving up."

Some people quoted Shakespeare. Richard quoted fashion designers.

"Yeah, well, your snooty designer buddy left all his money to a cat," I said. "If that isn't a sweatpants move, I don't know what is."

Richard inhaled sharply, but before he could zing one back to me, Kate flounced into my room wrapped up in a fluffy white robe. I made a mental note to make sure future hotels did not make more than one copy of my room key.

"You're dressed," she said, giving me the once-over. "I thought for sure you'd be neck deep in a bubble bath."

“I would be, but . . .” I flicked my eyes to Richard as he stood next to the bed with the hotel phone pressed to his ear giving our dinner order.

“Right,” she said, sinking onto the love seat. "I don't know if it's the jet lag or the whole dead body thing, but I'm wiped. And I just had to explain to one of our new brides back in DC that having bride and groom chairs that look like the Iron Throne is not a good idea, even if we could find a pair of them. It’s going to be enough of a challenge to find a string quartet that can play the *Game of Thrones* theme song for their processional."

"I would say I'm shocked anyone would want that, but nothing brides and grooms do shocks me anymore,” I said, walking over and joining her on the upholstered couch. “I am surprised you were able to pull yourself away from the cute garda long enough to return client calls."

"He had to leave." She poked out her lower lip. "They found something in one of the hedges and he tore out of the lobby. He did tell me not to leave the hotel though."

"He told all of us that," Richard said after he hung up the phone. "It's because we're potential suspects."

"Why would we have any reason to kill the woman?" Kate asked, crossing her legs and flashing most of one thigh. "Not only did we barely know her, we were together right before we found her."

"Maybe they think we're in on it together," I said.

"All four of us?" Kate leaned her head back to rest on the back of the love seat. "Like a gang?"

I tried to imagine the four of us as some sort of fussy, overly primped gang but couldn't do it. "You're right. No one would believe that."

"They would if Buster and Mack were here with us," Kate said. "When do they arrive?"

Our go-to floral duo were known for their cutting-edge designs as well as a personal style that evoked more Harley Davidson than Martha Stewart.

"Tomorrow," I said. "I hope we'll be cleared to leave by then."

"We've given our statements," Richard said. "And I hate to admit it, but Kate's right. None of us have motive or opportunity."

Kate smiled at Richard. "Thank you. You know, I'm right more often than you'd think."

"Don't push your luck, darling," Richard said.

The sharp raps on the door made me look down at my phone. "The service here is incredible. We ordered less than five minutes ago."

Richard walked across the room. "Those knocks do not sound like room service." He opened the door and Fern rushed in. "Like I was saying."

Fern staggered to one of the armless gray chairs in the raised alcove and sank into it. "Thank goodness I got here before they did."

"Before who got here?" I asked, straightening.

"The fuzz, the coppers, the police." Fern's eyes darted to the door, and he pulled a flask out of his pocket.

"You mean the Gardaí?" Richard asked.

Kate uncrossed her legs. "I wouldn't mind seeing one particular garda again."

"You would this time," Fern said, taking a swig from his flask. "They found what they think is the murder weapon."

"Really?" I said. "That's great. Why would that have anything to do with us?"

"Because," Fern tried to steady his breath as he waved at the scarf around his neck. "It's one of these."

"A scarf like that?" I studied the green Celtic symbols printed on the ivory background. "Didn't you buy that at the gift shop at Bunratty? I'm sure there are tons of places that sell them."

Fern shook his head and took another swig. "Not exactly like this one. A kelly-green one. Cashmere." He dropped his voice as if someone was listening in. "I saw the hot cop putting it in an evidence bag. It's exactly like the ones I gave each of you for this trip."

"Hand me the flask," Kate said.

So much for not getting sucked into the case.

❧ 11 ❧

"Are you positive?" I asked as I watched Fern lay his head on the round table between the two chairs and drape his arms over it. "It's Ireland. I'm sure there are lots of kelly-green scarves around. It's pretty much the country's color."

He lifted one arm to peek out from under it. "Of course I'm sure. They don't sell 100 percent cashmere in gift shops and certainly not Cesare Gatti."

"You named the scarves?" I asked.

"The designer, darling," Richard said with an exasperated huff. "The designer is Cesare Gatti, and they're available at Barney's."

"See?" Fern said, his voice muffled from under his arms. "They aren't just any old scarves. As if I would give you all just any old scarf." He lifted his arm again so I could see one eye. "And before you ask, I'm positive the scarf they found is one of ours, because I saw the label as the hot copper was putting it in the evidence bag."

"Just because it was one of our scarves doesn't mean we killed Colleen," Kate said, taking a sip from the flask Fern had handed her and grimacing. "Plus, no one knows it's one of ours."

"It will come out eventually," I said, knowing exactly what

Reese would say if he were here. "Better for us to be the ones to tell the Gardaí than someone else."

"Who else would tell them?" Kate asked.

Richard had begun pacing again, this time all the way across the room and back. "Oh, I don't know. Perhaps any of the old ladies who saw us wearing them."

I raised my hand. "Mine has been in my carry-on bag since the flight, so no one has seen me in one."

"I haven't taken mine out of its wrapping," Richard said, avoiding the dirty look Fern shot him with one eye and adding quickly, "I was waiting until the weather was cooler."

"That leaves you two," I said to Kate and Fern. "If we're positive the scarf they found is a Seymour Gatti, then it won't be hard to determine whose it is."

Fern groaned as if he were in pain then took the flask back from Kate. "Cesare, not Seymour. Let's not make this worse than it is, sweetie."

Kate jumped up and tightened the sash of her robe. "I'm all for getting this over with." She motioned to Fern with her head. "We need to locate our scarves to determine which one is missing."

I walked to the black Longchamp bag I'd dropped on the floor and dug through the contents. My fingers felt the soft roll of fabric tucked away at the bottom of the bag, and I pulled it out, holding the kelly-green scarf over my head. "Here is mine. Present and accounted for."

"And then there were three," Richard said.

Fern sat up, tucked the flask back into his pocket, and fluffed the Celtic scarf he wore like an ascot around his neck. "I know exactly where mine is. I switched it out with this one on the bus and rolled the other one up and put it in my Louis."

"Your Louis?" I asked. "Does everything you own have a name?"

"His Louis Vuitton duffel bag," Kate said under her breath.

"I'll show you." Fern led us out of my room and down the

hall to an identical door behind which was a room similar to mine but with two double beds instead of one king and no raised sitting area. Even though we'd only arrived a few hours earlier, the room already held Fern's unmistakable scent of high-end hair styling products.

Kate swiveled her head once we were inside. "You have two beds. I guess this is the room to use if we want to have a slumber party."

Fern's face lit up. "I'll do makeovers for everyone."

Richard cleared his throat. "One, we're here to find your scarf. Two, over my dead body are you giving me a makeover."

Fern mumbled something that sounded like "spoil sport" as he tossed aside the burgundy velvet throw pillow and placed his Louis Vuitton duffel bag on the gray upholstered chair. Zipping open the bag, he produced the green roll of cashmere from where it had indeed been tucked inside. "Voila."

"That's two," I said, glancing at Kate and Richard.

Richard spun on his heel. "Allow me to solve this mystery. Like I told you, my scarf never left my luggage."

Our procession left Fern's room, and we all traipsed back down the hall to Richard's room, Fern and I holding our scarves. He waved us into a room with one large window overlooking the lake and draped with floral curtains. His king-sized bed had a tall cream-colored headboard and was topped with blue velvet pillows each emblazoned with a large gold crown. More blue and gold crown pillows were perched on the blue velvet chairs that made up the sitting area at the foot of his bed, and a tufted blue velvet chair was tucked under the desk.

Richard strode to the closet and pulled out his black Gucci crossbody bag, opening the flap and holding out a green scarf still in the tissue paper with the fringe peeking out from one end. "Like I said. Unopened."

Fern sniffed and mumbled something as we all turned to Kate.

She tugged the front of her robe together with one hand.

"Impossible. My scarf should be in my Kate Spade bag. I wore it last night to dinner, and I'm almost positive I tucked it in there."

"I thought you had it on this morning on the minibus," I said, watching her face pale. "Didn't you wear it when we toured Bunratty Castle?"

She bit the edge of her lip. "I don't remember."

I put a hand on her arm. "Why don't we go look for it just to be sure?"

Kate nodded without answering, and we all walked from Richard's room to Kate's, which sat directly across from mine. A small sitting area with a round table and silver armless chairs led through an arch to the bedroom where Kate's black Kate Spade tote sat on the leather bench at the end of the king-sized four poster bed. Both the bed and the bench were buff colored with the only pop of color being the two maroon velvet roll pillows on the bed.

Kate rummaged around in her bag, her hands moving frantically until she upended the contents on the bench. Pens, an iPhone, a paperback mystery, and a hot-pink passport holder spilled out, but no kelly-green scarf.

She stepped back, shaking her head. "It was here. I know it was."

Fern wrapped an arm around her. "Just because it's missing doesn't mean you had anything to do with the old dear's death."

"Of course it doesn't," I said. What I left unsaid was what we all knew. It did pull our group deeper into the murder investigation, which was exactly what we didn't want to happen.

"Don't worry." I gave Kate what I hoped was my most reassuring smile. "This is circumstantial evidence at best. No one could suspect you of killing Colleen. You have no motive and you were with us up until we found her body."

"Well, I did pop down to the maze garden before we met up in the lobby," Kate said.

I felt my mouth drop. "You were outside before we went on our walk?"

"Just for a few minutes," Kate said. "I asked the front desk for their map of the grounds then went outside to the garden with the fountain and the low hedge designed like a maze. I thought it would be good for a fun Instagram pic."

"So the front desk gave you a map to the gardens and saw you leave by yourself?" Richard asked.

Kate nibbled the corner of her thumbnail. "Technically, yes."

Fern looked from me to Richard. "She still has no motive. She barely knew the woman. Both of you spent more time with her than Kate or I did."

I took both of Kate's hands in mine. "Is there anything else you can remember? Did you leave your scarf on the bus? Did you see someone near it? Did you see Colleen when you were outside? We need to know anything that could help us explain away this circumstantial evidence."

Kate shook her head. "I could have sworn I put the scarf in my bag, and I don't remember seeing anyone take it." She closed her eyes for a moment before opening them again. "I didn't see anyone when I was outside. It was only for a few minutes, then I walked back in and met you three in the lobby."

"What should we do?" Fern said, pulling out his flask again.

"As far as we know, the Gardaí haven't connected us to the scarf they think is the murder weapon. That gives us a little time to figure things out."

Richard crossed his arms. "What do you mean? I thought you swore up and down we weren't going to get sucked into another criminal investigation."

"That was before one of our scarves was used to kill someone. If there's even the slightest chance they could pin this on Kate, we have to figure out who's behind it."

Richard opened his mouth to protest, then sighed. "You're right. When I was falsely accused, you all rallied around me and did everything you could to prove my innocence."

I felt Kate's hands sag in mine.

"Thanks," she said as Fern pulled her close.

"For now, why don't we go back to my room and have dinner?" I said. "We'll all feel better once we've eaten."

We left Kate's room and headed across the hall to mine. I paused as I heard footsteps coming toward us and saw a pair of young men in hotel uniforms carrying large trays topped with silver domes.

"It looks like dinner has arrived," Richard said, holding my door open for the men to enter.

I breathed deeply as the plates were unloaded onto the coffee table. It had been hours since I'd eaten, and the smell of the food was a potent reminder. The men removed the silver domes with a flourish and turned to leave, but stopped in their tracks.

Garda Ryan stood in my doorway, his face serious. His eyes moved between us, and I realized that Fern, Richard, and I still held our green scarves. Kate's hands were empty. His gaze settled on her.

"Could I have a word?" he asked, his tone clearly indicating it would be unwise to refuse.

Kate looked at me, her face stricken, and for the first time in her life I knew she wasn't pleased to be propositioned by a handsome man.

12

"Are you still there?" I asked, holding my phone away from my ear to be sure I hadn't lost the call. Even though I could only hear a long exhalation of breath, the sound reassured me that my boyfriend was, in fact, still on the other end of the line. I tucked my legs up under me on the velvet love seat and eyed the untouched food set out on the coffee table. The room still held the lingering savory scents, but I wasn't in any mood to eat.

"I'm trying to process the fact that between the time I talked to you yesterday and now, you managed to get yourself involved in another murder investigation." Reese didn't sound angry, but I definitely recognized tones of disbelief.

"Would you believe me if I told you we were in the wrong place at the wrong time?" I kept my gaze firmly on the door in the hope that one of my friends would join me soon. The Gardaí had separated us in our rooms for more questioning, and the last time I'd poked my head into the hall, I'd been greeted by the female garda who seemed less than pleased to see me.

"Probably not," he said. "Didn't you just tell me that Kate's scarf was used as the murder weapon?"

"Yes, but obviously the real killer took it from her at some point." I picked up a limp chip from one of the plates.

"When is the last time Kate knows she had the scarf?" Reese had assumed his serious cop voice, and I could imagine him flipping open his notebook and jotting down information.

"She thinks she had it on the minibus when we traveled from Adare Manor to Dromoland Castle, but she can't be sure. She thought she put it in her carry-on tote bag, but she doesn't remember seeing it after getting on the bus."

"So it could have gone missing anytime between you all getting on the minibus with the tour group to arriving at the castle." Paper rustling accompanied Reese's voice. "Any of the ladies on the tour would have had access."

I nibbled on the end of the soggy chip and grimaced. Cold fries tasted bad no matter what you called them. "It doesn't make sense. Why would anyone want to kill an old lady they barely knew? It can't be a crime of passion. Most of these women had never laid eyes on each other before arriving in Ireland, and as far as I can tell, Colleen got along with everyone. It's not like it could be motivated by money either. I feel pretty confidant in saying that none of the other ladies on the tour are named in Colleen's will."

"There are other motivations for murder, babe."

"Well, I'm going to go out on a limb and say it wasn't about sex either. Aren't all crimes supposed to be about sex or money?"

"I think that's all fights between married couples," Reese said with a small chuckle. "There are more reasons people commit murder."

I felt my face warm at the mention of marriage again. Why did the thought of it make me so flustered? I dealt with marriage every day of the week. It was literally my job to help people get married. So why did I get nervous when my boyfriend just dropped the word?

"I doubt the Irish police seriously suspect Kate," Reese said. "It doesn't look great that her scarf was used to strangle the victim, but it won't take them long to determine that Kate had no connection to the woman."

I let myself sink back onto the couch cushions. "I hope you're right. I'm not used to dealing with cops I don't know."

"Or ones you can't sweet talk into not arresting you?"

I let out a small cry of indignation. "When did you have a reason to arrest me?"

"Would you like the list by date or severity of the crime?"

I folded my arms across my chest. "You know, it's a good thing you're so cute."

"I was thinking the exact same thing," he said, his voice becoming huskier. "How much longer are you going to be over there? The apartment feels lonely without you."

"Originally only a few more days, but that was before we found a body. We still need to visit all the castles on our client's list, so I hope the police here don't plan on keeping us."

"I'm sure if you explain that you're a wedding planner on a mission to find the perfect venue, they'll understand."

"I can hear the sarcasm in your voice, you know." I couldn't help grinning in spite of my desire to reach through the phone and throttle him.

"I'm sorry," he said, his voice more contrite. "I'm not trying to make light of the poor woman who died or of Kate's involvement. I'm sure she's upset to be connected to something so brutal."

"Don't forget Fern. He's the one who got us all matching scarves, and now one of them was used to commit a crime. He's pretty distraught."

"That a scarf was ruined or that a person was killed with it?" Reese asked.

He knew my friends too well. "It was cashmere and a designer label if that answers your question."

I heard voices in the background and the sound of a ringing phone. He must have been at the police precinct, which made sense considering it was the middle of the day back in DC.

"My best advice is to tell the police everything you know," he said. "The more information they have, the faster they can clear Kate and let you continue with your trip."

"The thing is we don't know that much, so I'm not sure how much help we can be. It's not like back home where we've known the victims and, in some cases, the killers. These people are complete strangers."

"To you, yes," he said. "But not to each other. There has to be a reason the woman was killed. It's not like she fell down a flight of stairs. No one accidentally gets strangled and pushed into a pond. Someone wanted her dead badly enough to kill her in broad daylight."

I rubbed my arms as a chill went through me. "I can't imagine any of those old ladies committing murder."

Reese laughed again. "Just because they look sweet? You know better than that. Some of the most devious killers have been the ones we've least expected."

That was true. I'd learned the hard way not to assume someone was innocent based on how they appeared. I sighed. "I wish you were here."

"Me too, babe, but you know I'm working the romance author murder." He dropped his voice, and I assumed he didn't want the other officers to hear him. "I'd much rather be with you in Ireland than riding around questioning witnesses with Hobbes."

"I thought he was in a better mood since he'd started dating Alexandra." Reese's partner and my favorite wedding cake designer had met when she'd been involved with one of our cases. I found the pairing of the glamorous European baker and the slightly doughy cop to be an odd matchup, but for some reason Alexandra found him charming.

"Oh, he's in a better mood. That's the problem." His voice became muffled, and I suspected he'd put his hand over the receiver. "He's acting like a lovesick puppy. I even caught him doodling her name the other day."

"Really?" Not what I would have expected from a DC detective in his forties. In contrast, Alexandra had been pretty tight-lipped about their relationship. Actually, she hadn't confirmed they were involved, but that wasn't surprising since Alexandra liked to keep an air of mystery around her. It paired well with her exotic accent and come-hither clothing.

"It could be worse," Reese said. "At least he doesn't give me a hard time about dating a woman who was originally a suspect in a murder case."

I drummed my fingers on the arm of the love seat. "This seems to be a recurring theme."

"Tell me about it," he said. "I just don't want to have to visit you or one of your buddies in an Irish prison."

I heard a commotion outside my door. "I promise you I'll try to stay out of trouble from now on."

"Promises, promises," my boyfriend said. "I'll be happy as long as I get you back home in one piece."

"Gotta run." I walked to the door. "I'll talk to you later."

"Love you, babe."

My heart fluttered in my chest. We'd only been saying the words to each other for a few months, and it still gave me a rush to hear it and to know he felt that way about me. "I love you too."

I disconnected as I heard the voices in the hall get louder. Chances were good it was either Fern or Richard pitching a fit about something. I knew I should intervene before one of them ended up in shackles.

I opened the door and stepped out into the hall, swiveling my head in the direction of the commotion.

"Annabelle!" It took me a moment to realize that the deep rumble of a voice belonged to Mack.

I gave a small shake of my head as I spotted him and Buster standing behind a pair of garda. As usual, the two burly men were decked out in black leather adorned with enough metal hardware and chains to make them rattle when they moved.

Both men had bald heads and goatees, and Buster wore motorcycle goggles as a headband.

"Mack? Is that you?" I slipped my phone into my pocket and hurried toward them. "I thought you weren't arriving until tomorrow."

The female garda angled her head at me. "You really know these men? They claim they're florists."

"That's right," I said. "They're a part of my wedding team."

She looked at them again and then at me. "Weddings?"

The leather of Buster's leather jacket creaked as he crossed his thick arms over his chest. "That's exactly what the people in customs said."

"I guess they don't get many male florists over here," Mack said.

I knew the general disbelief probably had more to do with the piercing in his eyebrow and the "Road Riders for Jesus" patch on his jacket than the fact that he was a man.

"I'm glad you made it." I pushed past the staring garda and gave them both a hug. "It's been a bit bumpy so far."

Mack cut his eyes to the uniformed officers. "I can see. Don't tell me it's another murder."

The two gardas exchanged a look, and I elbowed Mack. "It's all a big misunderstanding. Kate's being questioned now, but she's innocent."

"I don't know if that's the word I'd use to describe her," Richard said as he came up behind me, nodding to Buster and Mack.

"Remind me not to call any of you as character witnesses if I'm ever on trial," I muttered.

"I couldn't wait in my room another minute," Richard said. "Have they questioned you yet?"

I shook my head. "I assumed they were doing me last. I hope they haven't been with Kate this entire time."

As if on cue, the door to Kate's room opened and the handsome garda stepped out.

Mack inhaled sharply. "That's who was interviewing her?"

"I don't think we need to wonder why she's been in there so long," Richard said in a stage whisper, garnering him a dirty look from the female garda.

"I hope you're satisfied that our friend had nothing to do with the murder," I said as the tall garda approached our group.

Another door flew open, and Fern stepped into the hall with his arms outstretched and his wrists upturned. "Look no further. Lock me up. It's all my fault."

13

"Teaching women how to properly knot a scarf does not make you responsible if one of them gets strangled." I told Fern the next morning over breakfast.

We were seated in the Earl of Thomond restaurant surrounded by gilded wallpaper and oil paintings of distinguished-looking men. We'd already helped ourselves to the display of breakfast breads and fruits, and I was thrilled to find scones and strawberry jam in abundance. A waitress with fiery-red hair approached holding two full Irish breakfasts, and I could smell the sizzling sausages as she placed them in front of Buster and Mack.

I knew the full Irish breakfast consisted of fried eggs, bacon, sausages, baked beans, a grilled tomato, mushrooms, slices of black pudding, and toast. I also knew that I'd need an immediate nap if I ate that much in the morning.

"Here ye go, loves. The full Irish." The waitress gave them each a slow wink. "Can I get ye anything else?"

Mack blushed, and Buster shook his head with a daffy smile on his face. As they dug into their plates with gusto, I wondered if they knew that black pudding was a type of blood pudding. If they didn't, I wasn't going to be the one to tell them.

Fern eyed the hot plates as he picked at a piece of brown bread. "How do I know the murder just wasn't a Carmen Miranda gone wrong?"

"Is that a type of scarf knot?" I whispered to Kate, slathering sticky jam on a piece of scone and taking a bite.

She shrugged over the top of her teacup. "I mean, let's hope so."

Richard waved a fork with a strawberry on the end of it. "You must be out of your mind. If it was a knot gone wrong, why wasn't the scarf around her neck when we found her?"

Fern looked slightly mollified as he dabbed butter on his bread. "That's what the garda said last night when I tried to turn myself in." He paused in his buttering to blink away tears. "I still can't help thinking my tutorial might have sent someone down the wrong path."

Richard popped the strawberry into his mouth and shook his head as he chewed and swallowed. "Don't be silly. I may have felt homicidal after an hour of your scarf demonstration, but I still didn't murder anyone."

Fern reached over and squeezed his hand. "Aren't you a dear for saying so? That makes me feel better."

I shook my head in amazement and saw Mack grin.

Kate leaned back in her navy striped chair. "I don't know why you're worried. It's still my scarf that was used to kill Colleen, and we aren't any closer to figuring out who took it or why they wanted the little old lady dead."

"I would say that I'm shocked you were in Ireland for less than forty-eight hours without us and managed to stumble across a dead body, but that would be a lie," Mack said. "And you know I don't believe in lies."

Since Buster and Mack were part of a Christian motorcycle gang, they also didn't believe in cursing, cheating, or drinking.

Buster glanced at me as he cut into a silver dollar-sized piece of black pudding. "I'm surprised you haven't tried to solve it before the police."

"Oh, no you don't," Richard said, narrowing his eyes at the burly man. "The last thing Annabelle needs is a reason to start meddling. What we need to do is focus on our mission."

"This is tasty," Buster said after swallowing the blood sausage. "I wonder what's in black pudding."

Richard opened his mouth, no doubt to give a detailed description, and I jabbed the bread basket at him. "Brown bread?"

Fern glanced at Kate who looked equally confused. "Mission?"

Richard turned his ire from me and let his silverware clatter onto his plate. "To find the perfect wedding venue for our bride."

"I almost forgot about Hailey in the midst of all this murder business." Fern touched a hand to the ivory ascot at his neck, which looked remarkably similar to ones worn in the portraits on the wall. "You don't suppose she'll mind having her wedding in a place a woman was murdered, do you?"

"We aren't going to tell her," I said, making my voice more forceful than usual and looking around the table to catch everyone's eyes. "Right?"

They all nodded, although I could tell from Fern's expression that not spreading a story as juicy as this one would be a challenge.

"This is Ireland," Richard said. "I doubt we could find a castle where someone didn't die at some point in its history."

Now it was Fern's turn to drop his knife onto the table. "You don't think the castle is haunted, do you?"

"Of course not," I said at the same time Kate shrugged.

I shot her a look, which she ignored.

"If you ask me, all these really old buildings are probably haunted," Kate said. "Don't you remember the resort we visited in Pennsylvania? And that place wasn't half as old as this one."

Fern pressed his fingertips to his lips. "You're right." He dropped his hand and glanced around as if a ghost was about to leap out of the walls at him. "Maybe supernatural forces killed Colleen."

"Now there's a theory I'd like to see you float to the local Gardaí," Richard said. "As if they don't already think we're a bunch of crazy Americans."

"Speaking of which," Mack inclined his head at a group of women who'd entered the dining room. "I'm assuming they're in the genealogy tour group."

I recognized Betty Belle by her halo of white hair and her red-rimmed eyes. By her side was Nancy with the unnaturally red hair and arm full of shiny bangles that clinked as she moved, and the plump woman Betty Belle had referred to as Myrna's lackey. I couldn't remember the nondescript woman's name off the top of my head. All three women wore bright outfits, and Betty Belle's sweatshirt was a flag of Texas.

"What tipped you off?" Richard asked.

"I should go check on Betty Belle." I took a last crumbly bite of scone and stood. "She was Colleen's roommate, not to mention her closest friend on the trip."

The three women were adding sugar to their tea when I walked up, but only Betty Belle smiled when she saw me.

"Good morning, hon," Betty Belle said as she pulled apart a croissant. "I didn't know if we'd see you today after the big to-do last night."

"You mean the scarf?" I tried to keep my voice light.

The redhead's eyes widened. "Was that yours?"

"Don't you remember, Nancy?" Betty Belle said, nodding her head toward Kate. "It belongs to the blonde over there."

"But Kate had nothing to do with what happened to Colleen," I said quickly. "Someone stole her scarf from her during the day."

"Theft and murder." The third woman shook her head and her chin jiggled. "This type of thing has never happened on one of our trips before."

"That's right." I smiled at her. "This isn't your first trip to Ireland."

"Deb's been three times," Nancy said, fingering a chunky crystal hanging around her neck. "The same as me."

"You must love Ireland," I said. "Or just love traveling with Myrna."

"It's a thrill to track down your family roots," Deb said. "And Myrna's created a real community."

"I'm sure you're all distraught about what happened to Colleen," I said, watching their faces.

Betty Belle sniffled into her napkin, but the other two women only nodded.

"This was her first trip with us," Nancy said. "We didn't know her very well yet, but she was still part of our Facebook group family."

Deb buttered a scone as she peered up at me. "You and the jumpy fellow sat with her at dinner the other night, didn't you?"

I looked over my shoulder and saw that she meant Richard, who had indeed popped up from the table and was unfurling his napkin over the seat of his chair. "We did." I faced Betty Belle. "I didn't get to talk to her on the drive here though. You don't happen to know if something happened to upset her, do you?"

The white-haired woman tilted her head at me. "Upset her? Why, I don't think so. We split up at Bunratty Castle because I wanted to keep shopping and she wanted to return to the minibus, but she never mentioned anything. Why?"

"She said she wanted to talk to me after we arrived here. She didn't say what it was about, but she didn't show up where we'd agreed to meet, and the next time I saw her, she was dead."

"How awful." Betty Belle put a thickly veined hand to her cheek. "I can't imagine why she wanted to talk to you."

"Didn't she have a granddaughter getting married?" Deb asked the other two women. "Could it have been about that?"

Nancy twitched her shoulders up and down. "I didn't know her enough to know about her family."

"I don't remember her talking about a wedding," Betty Belle said. "But that could have been it. She does have a granddaughter."

I hadn't gotten the feeling she wanted to talk to me about wedding planning, but I didn't want to argue with the ladies.

Deb glanced down at her watch. "We'd better go if we want to make it to archery on time."

Betty Belle sighed as she pushed back her chair. "It feels wrong to be going along with the trip as if nothing happened."

"Now, honey," Nancy said, taking Betty Belle's hand as her bangles jangled around her wrist, "Colleen wouldn't have wanted you to spend the whole trip crying your eyes out."

Betty Belle dropped her purse then slowly bent to retrieve it, shuffling around the table and patting my arm. "I hope we'll see you later."

"The Gardaí haven't given us the okay to leave yet, so we'll be here," I told her.

The women left the dining room, and I glanced at their barely eaten breakfast. A flash of white on the floor next to Betty Belle's chair caught my eye. I walked closer and recognized the room key folder. She'd dropped her key. I picked it up and turned to chase after her, then stopped myself.

Betty Belle's room was also Colleen's room. There was a good chance Colleen's luggage was still in the room, as well as her carry-on and purse since they weren't with her when she was found. I knew it was a long shot that any of those items held a clue to her murder, but I felt an overwhelming desire to make sure. I knew what Reese would say, and I knew what Richard would say, but what I wanted most was to clear Kate and get back to our hunt for wedding venues. A quick peek at Colleen's belongings might help me do just that.

I looked over my shoulder at Richard as I slipped the key into my pocket. No way would he go along with sneaking into a hotel room. My eyes fell on Kate. Now she was another matter, especially if we could find something to clear her. She'd also gone along with some of my less-than-legal schemes in the past, so this wouldn't shock her.

Even if I got Kate on board, we'd need some way to distract Richard. It didn't take me more than a minute to settle on Fern. If anyone was born to create a distraction, it was him. I waited until Richard got up to go to the buffet before walking back to the breakfast table. Buster and Mack were debating soda bread versus scones, so they didn't pay much attention to me.

I leaned over Kate and whispered in her ear. "As soon as I give you the signal, you need to sneak out of here with me."

She gave a single nod, and I moved behind Fern. "When Richard comes back," I said low enough so only he could hear, "I need you to create a distraction so Kate and I can slip out."

He sat up straighter but didn't turn to face me. "Say no more, sweetie."

I took my seat and resumed sipping my now lukewarm tea. Richard took his seat next to me with another bowl of fruit.

"Well, would you believe it?" Fern jumped up and knocked his chair over and into Richard, which sent the fruit bowl into Richard's lap. "It's Derek and Grace."

Richard stood and chunks of fruit rolled off his pants and onto the floor. "My Burberry chinos!"

I pulled Kate to her feet and backed her away while Richard spluttered and Fern shrieked, running across the dining room toward a young couple. When we were out of the restaurant and halfway down the hall, I glanced behind us.

"No one can sell a story like Fern. Was he pretending to see the couple from the plane?"

"I don't think he was pretending, Annabelle," Kate said as she tried to keep up in her high-heeled boots. "Unless that husband and wife both have identical twins running around the country, that *was* the couple from the plane."

14

I glanced at the room number on the paper folder, grateful Betty Belle hadn't removed the key from it, and pulled Kate down the hallway after me. "What are the chances the same couple from the plane is staying here?"

"Pretty good since Fern gave them our itinerary," Kate reminded me.

My steps were quiet on the plush burgundy carpet, making the corridor seem even emptier. "Why would a couple come on their honeymoon without everything all planned out?"

Kate bobbled her head. "Maybe the groom was in charge of planning it and dropped the ball, or maybe they wanted to go where the wind took them."

I made a face. As a professional planner, I didn't understand the concept of winging it.

"Forget the couple for a moment." Kate grabbed my arm when I stopped in front of the correct room. "What are we doing?"

I realized that in the hurry to get out of the dining room without Richard noticing and the shock in realizing that Fern's distraction might not have been fabricated after all, I'd forgotten to explain my plan to Kate. I waved the key card at her. "Betty Belle dropped her room key."

Kate gave me a blank look.

I sighed. "She was Colleen's roommate. If Colleen's bags are still in the room, they may give us a clue as to why she was murdered."

Kate darted a glance down the hall. "What if she comes back to her room?"

"They have a group archery lesson right now. She'll be occupied for at least an hour." I inserted the key and the door opened. "If we don't find anything, we'll leave. No harm done."

My assistant didn't look so convinced. "Our hunts for clues haven't always gone so well in the past. I really don't want to get caught breaking and entering."

I looked up and down the hall again. Daylight streamed in the tall arched windows on one side, but the lamps glowed on the dark wood tables and illuminated the maroon walls. "No one will catch us. Don't you want to clear your name so we can get out of here? Hanging around until the Gardaí solve a murder is not on our itinerary."

"I know you don't like to get off schedule, but don't you think this is a bit extreme?"

"We'll be in and out in two minutes," I said, pushing open the door. "Promise."

Kate mumbled her weak protests as she followed me into the room. It didn't take me long to realize the layout was a suite with a sitting area that led into the bedroom through an open arch. The carpet was the same soft gray plaid as in my room, and the love seat and chairs were also gray velvet topped with burgundy throw pillows. A pair of beds took up most of the bedroom and held more burgundy pillows with a crystal chandelier hanging above. The room smelled like Betty Belle's perfume, a thick floral scent that made my nose twitch.

"How do we know which bags are Colleens?" Kate asked.

A hunter-green wheeled suitcase lay open on a luggage stand

near the bed, and a quilted floral tote bag sagged on the floor next to it. I scanned the room until I spotted a black wheeled suitcase tucked between the two high windows in the sitting area. A green nylon carry-on bag perched on top. "These haven't been opened. They must be Colleen's."

Kate pulled the smaller bag off. "What are we looking for?"

"I don't know," I admitted. "Something unusual? Something valuable? Something worth killing over?"

Kate gave me a look. "That's specific."

"I never said it wasn't a long shot."

Kate unzipped the bag and began rifling through it while I flipped the suitcase onto the floor. A green name tag in the shape of a shamrock hung from the bag's handle and confirmed that it belonged to the victim.

"Nothing in here," Kate said. "Tour guides, sunglasses, two tea towels, and one of those scarf brooches like Fern got--probably from the gift shop in Bunratty—her phone, wallet, and a passport case."

Before I could ask to see her phone, there was a sound at the door and we both froze. Kate dropped the carry-on bag next to the suitcase.

"She's back." Kate looked wildly around the room, but we were too far away to make it to any of the closets.

I motioned to the window seats. "Up there," I whispered. "Behind the curtains."

She gave me a look that told me she thought I was crazy, but jumped up and tugged the heavy drapes in front of her. I stood on the other side of the window with the long curtains shielding me from view, even though I could clearly see Kate's terrified expression across from me.

I put a finger to my lips as the door clicked open, and we heard someone entering the room. I didn't want to risk peeking out since the view from the door was straight at the windows, but the footfall sounded heavier than I would have expected from Betty Belle. My heart pounded, and I was sure the sound could be heard across the room. I squeezed my shaking hands tight and reminded myself not to lock my knees. We'd had more than one bridesmaid faint during a ceremony when they'd locked their knees and forgotten to breathe.

The thudding feet approached us, and I held my breath, even though I knew I shouldn't. Kate's eyes were squeezed shut, and she seemed to be mouthing something to herself. I hoped she wouldn't keel over onto the person. They were so close I could hear their rapid breathing. Either they'd run up the stairs from the lobby, or they were nervous to be in the room. Who was it if it wasn't Betty Belle? I fought the urge to look as I felt the curtain rustle as they brushed up against it. Chances were good if I looked out I'd be looking right at them. There was no good explanation for me to be huddled behind curtains on a windowsill. I didn't move.

I couldn't hold my breath any longer and tried to breathe out as quietly as possible, expecting the person to hear me at any moment. Instead of throwing back the drapes, they fumbled with the bags right below us, and then I heard the sound of the wheeled suitcase rolling across the carpet. Again, I wanted to look out, but common sense told me the risk of being seen was still too great. After another moment, the footsteps were gone and the door closed with a click.

I looked across the window seat. Kate's eyes were open and wide. I pulled the edge of the curtain back slightly. The room was empty, so I let my breath out in a long steady whoosh. "They're gone."

Kate peeked her head out from behind the brocade. "So are the bags."

My eyes went to the floor where we'd left the suitcase and carry-on bag. "The hotel staff must have retrieved them. I'm sure they're going back with the body."

"Or maybe the police want them," Kate said, not making a move to come down from the window. "You don't think that was Garda Ryan, do you?"

"I doubt it. I think he would have noticed something funny about the curtains. Whoever got the bags was in and out pretty fast." My phone buzzed, and I pulled it out of my pants pocket. "It's Richard."

"I guess he noticed we were gone."

I answered and tried to make my voice sound nonchalant. "Hey Richard. What's up?"

"I was about to ask you the same question."

"What do you mean? Kate and I decided to run up to our rooms to freshen up before our site tour."

"Your rooms?" Richard asked, doubt dripping from his voice. "You sure about that?"

"Pretty sure." I laughed but it sounded forced even to my own ears. Normally I would have assumed Fern had ratted us out, but he hadn't known where we were going.

"Turn around."

I pivoted in the window and gazed down at the stretch of lawn that extended along the lake. Richard stood below me, phone to his ear as he stared up at Kate and me standing in Betty Belle's window. "Oh."

Kate followed my line of sight and gave a small yelp. "I guess we should have figured standing in a giant window wasn't the most incognito option."

"I can explain," I began, but I stopped when I saw Fern join Richard and begin waving wildly up at us.

Kate waved back. "And so much for keeping this on the down low."

"Let's go," I told Kate, “before Fern starts selling tickets." I disconnected and jammed my phone back into my pocket. Kate and I needed to get out before anyone else spotted us, and I needed time to come up with a convincing explanation.

We jumped out of the window and hurriedly tied back the drapes. I wiped our footprints off the white surface of the window seats and scanned the room for any more clues we'd been there. Kate waved for me to follow her.

"Do you think anyone else saw us?" Kate asked after she'd crossed the room and stood listening at the door.

"I hope not." I placed the key card on the coffee table and joined her. "But we need to get out of here."

"Before Betty Belle finds us?"

I shook my head. "Before Richard does."

15

"You have to talk to me sometime," I said to Richard after the catering director had finished our tour of the castle and grounds and left us beneath the stone gazebo some distance away from the main building.

Richard turned away from me with a flip of his head. "Debatable."

Buster and Mack had insisted they wanted to take measurements in case our bride chose the gazebo for her ceremony and they needed to wrap floral garland around the soaring pillars. We'd all opted to remain outside with them while the catering director returned inside after warning us of impending rain. All except Fern, who'd practically danced inside at the thought of getting to wear his specially purchased rain gear.

I watched Richard stalk over to the gazebo and step up into the center. Knowing Richard the way I did, it was obvious he needed more time to cool off before he listened to the convincing argument I'd crafted in my head. Luckily, our tour had started before he could scold me for crouching in the windowsill of someone else's room. Once I could explain whose window Kate and I had been in and why, I felt sure he'd understand. At least I hoped he would.

"I've got it," Kate called down to Buster as she sat on his shoulders and held the extendable tape measure over her head.

"You think Hailey will prefer the gazebo to the walled garden?" I asked as Mack helped Kate down from Buster's shoulders. I felt grateful that for once Kate wore pants and not a skirt.

“This has a dramatic approach," Buster said, straightening his leather jacket once Kate was on the ground.

The long path leading to the domed open-air Temple of Mercury would make for a dramatic aisle, but the area surrounding it was more of a forest than gardens. Tall trees shaded the path and the stone was weathered with discolored patches and moss growing in places.

"The garden has more color," I said.

"You mean the garden where you found a dead body?" Mack shivered even though the mid-day sun peeked between the gray clouds and through the thick tree branches.

"Clearly we aren't going to mention the dead body," I said, looking from person to person. "Right?"

"Right," they all parroted back to me, although with less enthusiasm than I might have liked.

Buster looked over his shoulder at the long grassy approach from the side of the castle. "You can't beat the natural aisle."

"What about the other direction?" I asked, motioning to the more rustic path broken up by a set of crumbling stone steps.

Buster shook his head. "Too steep. We don't want guests rolling off their chairs.

Mack peered down at the tape measure and jotted some numbers into his notebook. "Just imagine if we draped fabric all the way down the lawn to the gazebo."

Kate brushed off the front of her snug-fitting black pants. "I'm not sure if Hailey is a fabric type of girl. What about ribbon streamers? They would flutter in the wind."

Mack beamed at her. "Brilliant." He dropped his head back to look at the figure perched on the top of the gazebo's dome. "You don't think we could get a floral garland on him, do you?"

Kate crossed her arms. "Well, I'm not crawling up there to put it on him."

As Mack and Buster debated the options for the Roman god, I wandered over to Richard.

"What do you think?" I asked. "Walled gardens or stone gazebo?"

"It's not like you'll listen to my advice," he said with a sniff as he turned to face away from me.

"Come on, Richard. You haven't even heard my explanation."

He spun around. "You have a reasonable explanation for why you and Kate were cowering in the windowsill of someone else's room?"

I put one hand on my hip. "First of all, we weren't cowering."

"Kate was hunched over with her eyes closed and her fingers crossed. What would you call that?"

I ignored his surprisingly accurate description of Kate. "How do you know that wasn't one of our rooms?"

He narrowed his eyes at me. "Our rooms are further down the hall, and I would hope you wouldn't have a reason to be hiding behind your own drapes. Luckily for you, I don't think Fern put two and two together."

"If you must know, we popped into Betty Belle's room. She left her key behind at breakfast, and I thought we might be able to find some clue in Colleen's luggage as to why she was murdered."

"I would ask you why you don't leave the police work to the police, but I know what an absurd question that is considering who I'm talking to." A pink flush crept up his neck. "What kind of clue did you expect to find in a dead woman's luggage?"

I felt my own face warm. "I wasn't sure, but I thought I should try before the Gardaí confiscated it or sent it back to the U.S. with her body."

"And how did that work out for you?" Richard tapped his foot on the stone.

"Not great," I said. "We barely started looking through

everything when someone else came in. That's why we jumped up onto the window seats."

Richard shook his head at me. "So you didn't even find anything? I don't suppose you thought about how you and Kate were going to explain yourselves if you got caught."

"We weren't supposed to get caught. Betty Belle and her entire tour group were at an archery lesson. Who else was going to walk into her room?"

"Maybe the hotel staff? Or the Gardaí?"

I gave him a look. "Well, I know that now. One of them must have come in for Colleen's luggage. It really wasn't our plan that was bad. It was just rotten timing."

Richard's eyes popped open. "Bad timing? You break into someone's hotel room to tamper with potential evidence and your only regret is bad timing? I have half a mind to call your boyfriend and tell him what you're up to."

I felt my stomach sink as I clutched his arm. "You can't. Reese would kill me."

"Maybe you'd listen to him," Richard said. "You certainly won't listen to me."

"You know that's not true," I said in my most placating tone of voice. "I listen to you all the time. Why do you think Wedding Belles has become so successful? It's because I took all your advice."

Richard frowned at me, but I could see a small smile threatening the corners of his mouth. "Nice try, darling. Of course it's true, but don't think you can sweet-talk your way out of this. And you don't take all my advice, otherwise you wouldn't be wearing boot cut jeans."

"I told her not to bring those," Kate said, joining us as Buster and Mack took a few more photos of the gazebo from further down on the lawn.

I tried not to roll my eyes at both of them. "Oh good, Brutus is chiming in."

Richard leveled a finger at her. "I'm still mad at you, by the way."

"You try to talk Annabelle out of something once she's set her mind to it. You know how she gets when there's a crime to solve or a problem to fix," Kate said, flipping her hair off her face. "Her superhero planner gene kicks in, and she's like a dog with a gnome."

Richard and I both stared at her.

"Do you mean a dog with a bone?" I asked.

She tapped a finger on her chin. "Maybe, but my version sounds more fun."

"I thought we agreed never to mention gnomes again?" Richard lowered his voice. "I still have nightmares about that you know."

One of our first weddings together had involved a couple that loved garden gnomes and insisted on including them in the buffet decor. Richard had agreed under great duress and claimed he'd never been the same since.

I shook my head. "That was five years ago."

"Might I remind you that I had to make accessories for said gnomes out of vegetables?" Richard said.

"Those carrot walking sticks were almost as impressive as the cauliflower hats," Kate said.

"Not helping," I said to her under my breath.

Buster and Mack lumbered toward us, Mack holding his notebook over his head. I glanced up at the sky and saw that the gray clouds had darkened and massed over us. Fat raindrops began falling from the sky as the two burly men ducked under the gazebo with us.

"Should we try to make a run for it before it gets too bad?" I asked, noticing a sliver of blue sky remaining over the castle.

"We're in leather," Mack said, gesturing at the head-to-toe black leather both men were in.

"Right." Since their leather was already stretched tight across their bulky bodies, I imagined by the time we made it to the castle their outfits might cut off their blood flow. "We'll have to wait it out then. Rainstorms pass quickly in Ireland, don't they?"

Richard's phone trilled in his pocket and he pulled it out, sighing with relief when he looked at the screen. "Thank heavens you called me back."

I raised an eyebrow at Kate and she shrugged. "Maybe the office manager at Richard Gerard Catering?"

"Were you able to measure him like I asked?" Richard said, pausing to listen before continuing. "The chest measurement is most important if the vest is going to fit him properly."

"Please tell me he's not talking about his dog," Kate whispered to me.

"His dog has a name," Richard said, giving Kate a pointed look. "I can't exactly get us custom-made tweed suits if I don't have the proper measurements."

I blinked a few times. "You're getting your dog a bespoke tweed suit?"

"I can't come home from a trip empty-handed now can I?" Richard gave me a look that told me *I* was the ridiculous one. "I forgot to bring him a present from Bali, and he nipped my ankles for a week."

"They already have matching pajamas, Annabelle," Kate reminded me. "Just go with it."

"We have to find a little something to bring home for Prue and Merry," Mack said, giving Buster a nudge. "Don't let me forget."

"I'm bringing home bottles of Irish whiskey for everyone," Kate said.

Mack put a hand to his chest. "We can't give whiskey to a teenager and a baby."

Buster and Mack had taken in Prue, an eighteen-year-old single mother, and her infant daughter, Merry, a few months earlier. Since then, Prue and Merry had lived above their flower shop in Georgetown while Prue finished high school, and Buster and Mack served as part-time caregivers. Despite their rough appearance, both men had taken to their role as stand-in fathers with gusto.

"What about Irish wool sweaters?" I suggested. "I'm going to get one for Reese."

"Should I get one for his brother so they'll match?" Kate asked.

"Daniel?" I said, trying not to stumble over my words. "Are you two dating?"

Keeping up with Kate's dating life was a full-time job, and I didn't even attempt it. My boyfriend's older brother was certainly handsome--dark good looks ran in the family--but he ran a private security company and had at least a decade on my assistant. Not that any of that was reason enough to dissuade her if she liked someone, but aside from some heavy flirting on her part, I hadn't even been aware they'd been seeing each other.

Before Kate could answer, we heard screams coming from across the lawn. I squinted to see through the rain as a figure in bright yellow ran toward us.

"Is that a construction worker?" Buster asked, his voice a low rumble over the pounding rain.

"Not even close," I said as I watched the person flail his arms. "It's Fern."

We stepped back as he reached the gazebo and ran under the dome, flipping back his hood and sucking in deep breaths. Now that he was close, I could see that he wore the kind of rain pants that hooked over your shoulders with suspenders and a jacket that reached mid thigh. He would have looked at home with the crew of *Deadliest Catch*.

"What on earth?" Richard asked, hanging up and joining us as we gathered around Fern.

"Had to come tell you," Fern gasped. "Couldn't wait."

"What happened?" I asked.

"Did your boat capsize?" Richard muttered.

Fern shot him a look as he shook his head and raindrops flew off his jacket. "Colleen's things are missing."

16

"Someone stole a dead woman's luggage?" Buster asked, shaking his head.

"Doesn't the hotel have it?" I asked. "I thought they'd retrieved it so it could be shipped back to her family."

Fern angled his head at me. "Where did you hear that?"

I exchanged a glance with Kate. I knew enough about law enforcement--no matter which side of the world it was on--to know if we revealed we'd been in the room when the luggage was taken, we'd catapult ourselves higher up the suspect list. Or get ourselves arrested. "I thought I heard something. Maybe I was wrong."

The rain blew in from the side of the open-air gazebo and stung my face. I pulled my arms around myself and shivered as thunder rumbled in the distance. When I'd imagined rain in Ireland, I hadn't envisioned it being such a cold, ominous downpour. The sky was the color of slate as sheets of rain lashed the dark gray castle, the turrets barely visible in the distance. I eyed Fern's full-body rain gear with longing.

"Who said it was stolen?" Kate asked, her voice raised over the pounding rain.

Fern stepped further under the gazebo until we all stood in

the very center facing each other. "Betty Belle noticed the luggage was missing when she went back to her room after archery."

I held my breath to see if Fern would make the connection to seeing us hiding in the window of a room at the same time Colleen's luggage was taken. "And no one saw anything suspicious?"

I ignored the pointed look Richard shot me.

"Not a thing," Fern said. "The hotel swears up and down they didn't send a bellman to get it, and the Gardaí say they didn't confiscate it."

I bit the edge of my lip. "The Gardaí are involved already?"

Kate smiled and touched a hand to her hair. "They're here?"

Fern nodded. "The hotel called them. I think the staff is afraid of being blamed for losing the dead woman's belongings as well as being the place she was murdered."

I glanced across the lawn leading to the castle, hoping I wouldn't see officers heading our way. I didn't trust Kate not to cave under questioning from the cute garda.

"I'm starting to have second thoughts about this place for the wedding," Mack said.

"Do you think it's haunted too?" Fern asked.

Richard let out an exasperated breath. "Not this again."

Fern pulled himself up to his full height. "Plenty of castles over here are haunted. It's common knowledge. I'm not saying the spirits at Dromoland are evil, but they may like to cause trouble by moving things around."

"I hope you're not suggesting that a ghost stole Colleen's luggage," Richard said.

Fern twitched one shoulder. "I don't think we should discount it as a possibility."

Richard muttered something to himself, and I was glad the storm was loud enough to drown him out. I doubted Fern would have come out on the winning end of his comments.

"Even if the castle has some friendly spirits hanging around, I doubt they could move a suitcase," I said.

Fern drummed his fingers across his lips. "Annabelle's right. It's rare for a spirit to take a corporeal form solid enough to move matter."

"And why would a ghost want to take Colleen's luggage?" I asked. "It doesn't make any sense."

Fern's shoulders sagged. "I suppose you're right."

"Why would anyone want to take the dead woman's luggage?" Mack asked. I could tell from his expression he was glad we were off the topic of ghosts and spirits.

"It has to be the person who killed her," I said, rubbing my hands briskly over my arms to warm them up. "They must think the bags contain some sort of evidence."

Kate stared at me, and I knew she was thinking the same thing I was. If the killer was the person who took the bags, then we'd been inches away from them. I could have kicked myself for not getting a look before they left the room.

"It has to be someone in the tour group," Kate said. "No one else knew Colleen, and she didn't seem like the type to inspire a crime of passion."

Fern sucked in air. "You think one of those sweet old ladies killed her?"

"Just because they're old doesn't mean they're sweet," Buster said.

Mack bobbed his head in agreement. "We've done the decor for lots of Colonial Dames luncheons, and I've seen them rip people to bits over creases in tablecloths."

Kate nudged me. "Remember that grandmother who body checked the mother of the bride to get a better view of the processional? And how many grabby grandpas have we had to fend off?"

"I think we can all agree old age doesn't make a person necessarily nicer," I said. "None of the women in the genealogy tour seem capable of murder to me, but I don't know them very well either."

"I, for one, do not want to know them well," Richard said. "We need to focus on getting out of here and away from all the crazies. We still have castles to visit and a flight from Dublin in a few days. That means no more theorizing about suspects or meddling in the murder investigation."

I knew his statement was directed almost solely at me. "Fine. Let's just hope the Gardaí see their way to let us leave."

Fern stepped to the edge of the gazebo and stretched out his arm. "At least the rain is slowing down. I thought we might be stuck out here all day. Well, I thought you all might be stuck out here all day, since I'm the only one dressed for the weather."

The clouds above the castle had parted and slivers of blue peeked through the clouds. Even though the rain hadn't stopped, the drops were slowing.

"I'm going to make a dash for it," I said, placing the Dromoland sales folder over my head. "I still need to send Hailey the latest photos and check emails."

"You might need to wait on that," Fern said as we set out across the lawn. "The police are going room to room looking for the missing luggage. Everyone's waiting in the lobby to be cleared to return to their room."

"Just what I need." Richard lifted his feet high in the wet grass. "People pawing through my clothes with no awareness of how to handle expensive fabrics."

"You don't think they'll go through all our things, do you?" Kate asked, making me wonder what exactly she'd packed that made her look so nervous.

"Consider yourself lucky," Richard cast a glance at Buster and Mack. "It's hard to manhandle leather."

Mack touched the "Ride Hard Die Saved" patch on the front of his black jacket, and I got the feeling he didn't agree with Richard's assessment.

"If they're looking for the missing bags, I'm sure they'll be looking for someone who stashed those away. I doubt they want to search our drawers." I felt my feet sink into the soggy ground and hoped my black flats weren't going to be ruined. In an effort to pack light, I'd only brought two pairs of shoes, a move I currently regretted.

We reached the side of the castle, and I felt grateful to be off the wet grass. I tried to scrape the dirt and mud off my shoes as we walked up the steps to the front entrance, stopping at the wide front door and hesitating when I saw the crowded lobby. It looked like every chair, love seat, and spot along the wall was taken by a disgruntled-looking guest.

"This may have been a mistake," Richard whispered to me as all eyes swiveled to us.

I recognized the tall handsome garda as he approached with the blond female garda close behind, wearing a triumphant look on her face. "Garda Ryan. Nice to see you again."

He didn't return my smile. Instead he held out a latex-gloved hand and the green shamrock luggage tag resting in his palm. "Do you recognize this?"

"Isn't it the luggage tags for the genealogy tour group?" I asked.

He flicked his eyes to me. "I wasn't asking you. I was asking Kate."

"Me?" Kate's mouth dropped open. "Why?"

The garda turned it over to reveal the name written on the other side. "Because it belonged to the deceased, and it was found on the floor of your room."

"What?" Kate blinked at it a few times. "Why would it be in my room?"

Garda Ryan stared at her until her mouth dropped open.

"Wait, you think I took Colleen's luggage?" she asked. "Why would I do that?"

The blond garda folded her arms across her chest and grinned. I put a hand on Kate's arm so she wouldn't say anything that might make her look bad.

"If you think Kate dragged some other lady's luggage around, then you don't know her very well," Richard said. "She doesn't even move her own luggage."

"That's right," Fern said, leaning close to the green tag sitting in the garda's palm. "Although I wouldn't blame her for ripping that luggage tag off. Is that plastic?"

"Thanks," I whispered to both of them. "Very helpful."

"I do what I can," Richard said.

"Why were you searching her room?" I asked. "Did you have a warrant?"

I wasn't sure how searches and warrants worked in Ireland, but Garda Ryan didn't seem bothered by my questions.

"Kate is a suspect because of her connection to the murder weapon," he said. "It was a natural step to search her room in case she was also involved in the latest crime."

Buster stepped forward, looming over the garda even though the Irishman wasn't short. "Kate didn't commit any crime."

"That's right," Mack added, stepping up to flank Kate. "Our friend may break her share of hearts, but she would never kill anyone or steal their luggage."

Kate sniffled. "Thanks, guys."

"Where exactly did you find this luggage tag anyway?" I asked.

Before Garda Ryan could answer, the blonde behind him said, "On the floor."

"Near the door?" I asked.

"No," she said, looking smug. "A few feet inside."

Garda Ryan turned and shot daggers at her, and the woman's triumphant look faded.

"Thank you," I said to her, giving her my sweetest smile. "That's very helpful."

"Would you like to give us a statement?" the garda said when he turned back around and focused on Kate.

I shook my head. "I don't think that's a good idea."

"That's right." Fern hooked his arm through hers. "My client needs to confer with counsel before speaking with you."

Both officers looked confused as Fern turned and pulled Kate away. Fern looked back at me and lowered his voice. "I knew I should have packed my barrister wig."

17

"Obviously she's being framed," I said, cupping my hand over the bottom of my cell phone as I pushed open the door to my room, noticing the maid's cart a few doors down and hearing the hum of a distant vacuum cleaner. Fern was off calming Kate down while I had agreed to put in a call to "counsel."

"I tend to believe you," my boyfriend said from the other end of the line, "but that's only because I know Kate, and I know she's only a predator when it comes to dating."

"Exactly," I said, not sure if that was completely flattering to Kate but deciding not to debate the point.

I flopped onto the love seat at the end of the bed and kicked off my black flats.

"Tell me again about the luggage tag," Reese asked.

"All the women on the tour have them attached to their luggage. I'm assuming so they can find their bags more easily, or it's part of their trip swag." I shivered in my still-damp clothes. "They're green pleather and shaped like shamrocks and have the name of their genealogy Facebook group on one side."

"So not something you could pick up anywhere?" Reese asked.

"Not really. I haven't asked, but I assumed they got them before they left the U.S."

"That would make sense."

I heard the sound of a door opening on his end and then a bottle being opened. "Are you at home?"

"I just got in from pulling a double shift." He swallowed. "I'm beat."

"Are you drinking a beer?" I asked, doing a quick time zone calculation in my head. "Isn't it morning there?"

"Sure is. I have big plans to finish this beer and sleep the rest of the day."

"Do you want me to let you go?" I asked. "If you're too tired to talk . . ."

"Babe," he cut me off, "I'm never too tired for you. Let's go over this again. Did the officer say where they found it in Kate's room?"

"No, just that it was on the floor." I rubbed my palm over my forehead. "The person who stole Colleen's luggage must have managed to sneak into Kate's room afterward and plant the tag."

"How do you know the tag was on the victim's luggage when it was taken? It could have been taken off at an earlier point."

"Because I saw it on both of her bags right before they went missing," I said before thinking better of it.

"I thought you said the bags disappeared from the victim's room."

Crap. Sometimes I forgot that my boyfriend was paid to notice inconsistencies in witness statements.

"Annabelle?" His voice was serious. "What aren't you telling me?"

"Nothing important," I said. "At least nothing that relates to the murder."

Another long swallow. "Why am I having a hard time believing you?"

"Because you're a naturally suspicious person who deals with criminals on a daily basis," I suggested.

"Or because I know you can't stop yourself from trying to fix any problem, and you consider this murder case a problem."

I didn't know whether I should be flattered he knew me so well or annoyed that he had me pegged. I waited a few beats, but he didn't say anything. Reese was also a pro at interrogation, and he could always wait me out. I knew I wouldn't be doing myself any favors by confessing my latest misdeed, but I also hated the idea of keeping things from him. Not like my lack of control when it came to solving crimes would come as a surprise to him.

"Fine," I said with a loud exhalation. "Kate and I popped into Betty Belle and Colleen's room. We were about to look through Colleen's bags when someone startled us."

Another long pause. "How did you get into the room?"

"A key," I said, not volunteering any more than that.

"I'm assuming you weren't given the key, but I'm going to put a pin in that for now. What happened when someone walked in on you searching the bags?"

"We hid so they didn't see us. Unfortunately, we also didn't see them when they left with the bags."

Reese sighed. "I'm going to take a wild guess that you haven't shared this with the Irish police?"

"It doesn't make us look very good," I said.

"It makes you look a little crazy." I could hear the irritation in his voice. "Hold on. Someone won't stop knocking on the door."

Before I could advise him to turn off all the lights and hide under the bed, I heard the distinctive sound of Leatrice's voice accompanied by dog barks. Too late.

"Do you need to go?" I asked, not eager to be lectured by my boyfriend on meddling in an investigation.

"Don't even dream of hanging up on me," he said, his voice low and muffled. "We definitely aren't done."

I looked over to the alarm clock on the bedside table. I needed to get back to my friends soon.

"Annabelle, dear," Leatrice said through the phone. "Is that you?"

"It's me," I said, trying to sound upbeat. "How are things over there?"

"Well, I think I may have figured out how some of the spies in our area are passing messages."

Leatrice considered herself a one-woman neighborhood watch and amateur secret agent all rolled into one.

"Really? When you say 'our area' do you mean Georgetown or greater Washington DC?"

"Georgetown," Leatrice whispered. "You know this area has the highest concentration of sleeper spies of any place on the planet, don't you?"

I wasn't sure how she'd verified her information, but I decided not to ask.

"I think they're doing it with dog poo," she said.

"I beg your pardon?"

"You know the plastic bags of poo people sometimes leave on the sidewalk or drop into trash cans? I think those are actually decoys. What better way to pass messages that no one else will intercept?"

I closed my eyes. "Please tell me you aren't gathering other people's dog poo."

"Not yet," she said.

"I thought the wedding planning would keep you too busy to worry about all that spy stuff anymore." Hoped was probably more like it.

"The wedding planning has been put on hold until you all come back home," she said. "Isn't that right, love muffin?"

I guessed that meant Sidney Allen was with her, which meant Leatrice, her fiancé, and Richard's dog were all in the apartment with Reese. I stifled a laugh.

"Just because we're gone doesn't mean you can take a break, " I said. "Especially if you want a short engagement. You should be looking for your dress and finalizing your guest list and bridal party, if you intend to have one."

Hermès yipped in the background. "I had no idea. Fern didn't give me a timeline."

"He's not big on them. He's more of a big ideas person," I said. "Speaking of big ideas, I convinced him to drop the murder mystery theme. Sidney Allen does not have to spend his wedding day pretending to be a corpse."

Leatrice gave a little whoop. "Thank you, dear. Fern doesn't hate me, does he?"

"Of course not. He's already forgotten about it." I didn't tell her that he'd forgotten about it because we were knee-deep in another murder. "But you should start looking for your dress before we get home. Unless you find something off-the-rack, they can take a while to order. There are a couple of bridal shops in Georgetown you can check out."

"Okay, but I'll wait until you and Kate are back to pick out bridesmaids' dresses. I want you to pick something you like."

Even though we were thousands of miles apart, I felt my face freeze. "You want us to be bridesmaids?"

"Didn't you know that? It wouldn't be the same without you and Kate standing by my side."

Even though a part of me was touched, another part of me was horrified at the thought of being a bridesmaid. I was used to being on the other side of things and behind the scenes. The thought of standing at the front of the ceremony made my palms sweaty.

"I like the idea of all of the ladies wearing lace jumpsuits," Leatrice continued. "I'd be in white, obviously, but do you think they have them in orange for you girls?"

My mouth went dry.

"Hey babe," Reese's voice came back on the phone. "I was going to give you a hard time about what you've been up to, but after what Leatrice just told you, I think it would be cruel."

"She's joking about orange lace jumpsuits, right?" I said.

"To give you a little perspective, she's currently wearing a double knit green pantsuit with a spread collar." He paused. "And her earrings light up."

I took a deep breath and told myself it wasn't the end of the world. Maybe being detained in Ireland indefinitely wasn't such a bad idea. I saw something fly across the floor from the doorway. "Hold on a second."

The white square came to rest a few feet inside my room, and I walked over to retrieve it. It appeared to be a note written on hotel stationery and folded several times. I recognized Fern's loopy handwriting.

Meet us in the parking lot in five minutes.

I shook my head. Knowing Fern, he was planning a full-scale-style departure.

"Everything okay?" Reese asked. "Or are you still recovering from the idea of orange lace?"

"I've decided to worry about that later. I think I may have an idea about the case though." I looked at the note then at the floor. Finally, I dropped to my knees and eyed the bottom of the hotel door. "I think I figured out how someone is framing Kate. At least part of it."

"That was fast. Was it something I said?"

"Actually, I think I have Fern to thank," I said.

"That might be a first," Reese said with a laugh.

I opened my door and spotted Fern moving down the hall. He'd traded in his hard-core weather gear for a trench coat and dark sunglasses.

He spun around when he heard me and peered down over the glasses. "Did you read my note? Are you ready to break out of here?"

"I just have to talk to the Gardaí first," I said. "Then I think they might be happy to let us go."

18

"What's all this about you poking a hole in my case?" Garda Ryan asked, tapping one foot on the carpeted floor of Kate's room.

I'd asked Fern to bring him up while I gathered the rest of our team in Kate's room, and now we all stood inside the small sitting area. I'd also asked Betty Belle for the use of her green shamrock luggage tag, so she stood with us looking slightly confused and a bit weepy.

Kate sat on one of the silver upholstered chairs with Fern, still in his trench coat and sunglasses, by her side.

"This is very Hercule Poirot," Richard said. "I hope you know what you're doing, darling."

"Me too," I whispered. I wasn't thrilled the female garda who seemed to have a grudge against Kate had joined us, but I also couldn't think of a reason to kick her out.

Buster shifted from one foot to the next and his leather pants creaked. "You don't need to prove anything to us."

"That's right," Mack said, shooting both gardas dirty looks. "Anyone who knows Kate knows she's innocent."

"Exactly," I said. "We're here to show that Kate is innocent and prove she's being framed."

The gardas exchanged a glance that told me I needed to speed up my dramatic reveal before I lost them.

I held up the shamrock luggage tag. "This is an exact copy of the luggage tag you claim to have found on the floor of Kate's room. Is that correct?"

The blond garda let out an impatient huff. "You know it is."

I looked at Garda Ryan until he nodded his agreement. I glanced back at the female garda. "Since you were kind enough to tell us that it was found a few feet inside her hotel room door, I thought we might try an experiment." I walked to the hotel door and opened it, stepping out into the hall. "I assert that the person who wanted to frame Kate actually threw the tag under the door." I pointed to the bottom of the door. "You'll notice that the door sits off the carpet at least an inch."

Garda Ryan raised an eyebrow and he bent down on his haunches, eyeing the bottom of the door. "That it does."

"Let's give it a try," I said, closing the door so that I was in the hallway alone. I rubbed my thumb across the textured surface of the tag and closed my eyes for a beat, whispering to myself, "This had better work."

I bent down with my heart beating fast and flicked the tag under the door as hard as I could. I waited a second, releasing the breath I'd been holding without even realizing it, and knocked.

Richard opened the door, beaming at me. "Nicely done, inspector."

Both gardas stood looking down at where the luggage tag lay several feet inside the room. The blonde flicked her eyes nervously from the tag to her boss, and I knew that I'd hit the mark. I felt a flood of relief as I saw Kate grinning at me.

"Look how far it flew," Betty Belle said, her voice holding tones of surprise. "I never would have thought of doing that."

Mack patted her arm. "You don't have a criminal mind."

"I guess I don't," the white-haired lady said in her Texas drawl.

Garda Ryan picked up the green shamrock. "This doesn't prove she's innocent."

"But it does show how easily someone else could have planted the tag in her room. You can't say without a doubt that Kate ever had the luggage tag in her possession." I held his gaze. "It actually seems more than likely that she's being set up, because only an idiot would use their own scarf to kill someone and leave it behind to be found, and then drop the victim's luggage tag in the middle of their room."

"Annabelle's right," Fern said. "Neither of those are something a real criminal would do if they were guilty. Trust us, we've gone up against plenty of criminals."

Kate stood. "I told you I had nothing to do with Colleen's death or her luggage disappearing. What's my motive?"

"You're all Americans," the blonde said.

"That's hardly a motive, dear," Richard said. "We aren't quite as homicidal as you might think. Well, not all of us."

The woman's pupils widened as Richard arched a brow at her.

"So," I said, my eyes focused on the cute garda whose cheeks were now flushed pink, “unless you have any legitimate objections, we're going to go check out another historic venue."

"As long as you aren't checking out," he said, his voice not as authoritative as it had been.

"Not yet," I said, "but if I were you, I'd focus on finding the real killer. If we poked a hole in your case against Kate this easily, just think what a lawyer would do."

"That's right," Fern told him. "You do not want to see me when I'm in my full barrister costume."

"A real lawyer," I muttered to Fern as we walked out of the room and down the hall.

He shrugged. "Never underestimate the power of a good wig, sweetie."

"Thanks, Annie," Kate said, slipping an arm around me. "You were brilliant."

"Don't tell Fern," I said, keeping my voice low as he walked ahead of me. "He's the one who gave me the idea by flicking a note under my door. It made me really look at the doors and realize they're cut higher off the carpet than usual, making it easy to slide things under. Even thick things like a luggage tag."

"I hope you got it out of your system," Richard said, walking in step with us.

"Got what out of my system?" I asked.

"You know." He circled his hand at the wrist. "Solving crimes. I hope this means we can move on without you insisting on tracking down the killer. We are here to find a wedding venue, you know."

"I know," I said. "As long as none of us are being framed for murder, I'm perfectly happy letting the Gardaí take care of finding Colleen's killer."

Richard patted his pockets. "Who has a pen? I need to get this in writing."

"Hilarious," I said. "I promise you I have no desire to spend the rest of our trip embroiled in an investigation. We're leaving to see another venue. Would I do that if I were obsessed with solving the case?"

Richard mumbled something I couldn't quite make out as Fern waved us toward a side door.

"I had the driver idle the van in the parking lot so he'd be ready for us when we escaped," Fern said. "He also stocked the van with bottled waters and snacks."

"What would a breakout be without snacks?" Kate asked.

"You know I always go on the lam in style, sweetie," Fern said, slipping his sunglasses down and popping the collar of his trench coat.

19

"I'm not sure if this is considered a breakout if it's sanctioned by the Gardaí," Richard said as we settled ourselves in the front seat of the minibus and the engine rumbled to life.

"It gets us out of the castle, and we can check two more venues off our list." I put my black nylon tote on the floor and sank back against the fabric seats, glad not to be leaning against the stone wall of the lobby and flanked by cold metal suits of armor. "Glenlo Abbey Hotel is a second-string option, and I don't think Hailey will want to have her ceremony on the Cliffs of Moher, but at least we can give her the options. I don't relish telling the senator we couldn't visit all the venues because we were being detained as murder suspects."

Richard held up a finger. "Technically, only Kate is a suspect."

"As if we'd leave her behind," I said, giving him a scathing look. "It's all for one and one for all."

Fern plopped down in the seat across the aisle from us and directly behind the driver. "I've always wanted to be one of the three musketeers, especially if we could have matching capes."

"No capes," Richard said before the words were completely out of Fern's mouth.

"Spoil sport," Kate said, sliding in next to Fern and giving me a wink and a paper to-go cup. "But thanks for the sentiment, Annabelle."

I breathed in the scent of coffee from the lid of the to-go cup and smiled at her, thrilled to have a liquid pick-me-up and happy she was no longer being questioned by the Gardaí. Somehow she'd managed not to let slip that we'd been inside Betty Belle's room, and I knew I owed her big time. For that and the coffee. Knowing Kate, a few Friday nights off to go on dates instead of working wedding rehearsals with me would be the perfect reward.

I took a sip. It wasn't my usual mocha, but it would do. Twisting around to look at the older women scattered throughout the rest of the fifteen-seater, I spotted Buster and Mack taking up the entire back seat. I gave them a wave. "How many more people are joining us on our search for the perfect wedding venue?"

"I couldn't exactly hijack their driver without inviting them, could I now?" Fern whispered, taking a swig from his own paper cup. "Not everyone wanted to come. Betty Belle is still upset about Colleen, and now she's newly upset that someone broke into their room and took Colleen's luggage."

Nancy passed us and a cloud of patchouli followed her. Combined with the Bengay and floral perfumes of the other ladies, the smell made my eyes water. I lowered my window.

"So we'll have a little space to spread out?" Richard eyeballed me and the empty seats behind me.

Fern's cheeks flushed. "Since we had some people decline, I didn't think it would be a problem to extend the invitation."

"Extend the invitation?" Richard asked. "To whom? Don't tell me the handsome garda is coming as a personal security escort for Kate."

Kate sat up. "I wouldn't mind that."

"It's Derek and Grace," Fern said. "From the plane."

"They're still here?" I asked. "I thought they'd just come to the castle to visit the grounds."

"They did," Fern said with a flutter of his hand. "I couldn't exactly plan an outing to Glenlo Abbey and the Cliffs of Moher without at least seeing if they'd like to join us."

"Couldn't you?" Richard mumbled.

Before I could ask Fern more about the couple who'd happened to show up at our hotel, the newlyweds walked onto the bus.

"Hi everyone," Grace said, giving a finger wave. "Thanks for letting us tag along."

Her husband followed her, grinning and nodding as they made their way to two empty seats in the middle of the bus. I noticed he was about a foot taller than his wife and had short brown hair in contrast to her curly blond hair that bounced as she walked. It might have been her walk that was bouncier than her hair, since she struck me as being very perky.

Fern tapped the bus driver's shoulder. "That's everyone, Seamus."

Richard raised an eyebrow at me as the bus shifted into gear and jerked forward. "It's not too late to jump off."

"And stay at the castle even longer?" I shook my head. "I'll take my chances being cooped up with the newlyweds."

Fern took my coffee from me, glanced around the bus furtively, and slipped a silver flask from the inside pocket of his blazer. "This will take the edge off, sweetie."

I eyed his coffee cup. "Am I to assume you don't have coffee in your cup?"

He gave me a scandalized look. "Of course I do. It's just Irish coffee." He winked at me as he poured a stream of amber liquid into my coffee. "When in Rome, you know."

I took the augmented drink from him and took a tiny sip, flinching at the kick it now had. "This should do it."

I sat back and closed my eyes as we drove out of the Dromoland estate, knowing we had about an hour on the highway until we reached Glenlo Abbey. I hadn't slept well the night before. Images of Colleen floating among the lily pads had haunted my dreams, and worry about Kate had made what sleep I had gotten fitful at best. I took another longer drink and let the warmth of the coffee and Irish whiskey relax me.

I wasn't sure how long I'd been dozing when snatches of conversation pulled me out. I looked out the front window and saw that we were no longer on the highway. The road was now two lanes with tall trees on either side.

"Of course Kate is being framed," Fern said. "Why would she have strangled Colleen with her own scarf?"

"Why would I strangle Colleen in the first place?" Kate added.

"Too true, sweetie," Fern said. "Too true."

I rubbed my eyes as I sat up, elbowing Richard beside me. "How close are we?"

"Close," he said. "You slept through the discussions of bangs and the Pantone color of the year. Believe me, you didn't miss a thing."

I swiveled to see who Fern and Kate were talking to and saw that the perky bride and her nondescript yet smiley groom were leaning out into the aisle hanging on every word.

"So someone stole your scarf and then killed a woman with it?" Grace's blue eyes were so big they seemed to take up most of her face. "Who would do such a thing?"

"It couldn't have been anyone who knew her."

I recognized Nancy's voice from the back and twisted to see her bright-red hair popping into the aisle.

"If you ask me," Nancy said, “there's a maniac on the loose."

Murmurs passed through the bus.

Fern sucked in his breath. "I hadn't even thought of that."

"Why do you think I came today?" Nancy asked. "You wouldn't catch me wandering around the castle by myself. Not after poor Colleen. I don't blame her for being so jittery when we got to the castle. She told me she had an uneasy feeling."

I thought back to Colleen’s comments when we'd gotten off

the bus at Dromoland. She'd seemed nervous, but I hadn't known why.

"Ghosts," Fern said and nudged Kate with a knowing nod of his head.

I noticed that his voice was a bit slurred and made a mental note to confiscate his flask before he started seeing spirits floating through every castle we visited.

"Maybe a maniac ghost," Kate said.

Richard gave a derisive snort next to me.

"You think her uneasy feeling had to do with a premonition she'd be murdered?" Grace asked.

Nancy shrugged and her long crystal earrings brushed her shoulders. "All I know is she'd been acting odd all morning and talking nonsense. Some people are more attuned to energy than others. Colleen may have sensed something before it happened."

The bus turned up a drive, and we approached the dove-gray square building with an attached turreted tower. A wide staircase swept up the front of the building, and a small fountain sat across from the entrance surrounded by tidy hedges and bursts of flowering shrubs.

"It's pretty," Kate said, "but it looks small."

I had to agree with her. Knowing our bride, she would prefer the flash of Dromoland Castle to the charm of a restored home with an attached abbey.

"It extends further to the back," Richard said, craning his neck as we parked. "And the Orient Express Pullman carriages are off to one side."

"The Orient Express?" Fern's voice was hushed as he stared at Richard. "As in *Murder on the Orient Express?*"

"As in the hotel acquired two of the original carriages and restored them so they now serve as a restaurant," Richard said, reading from his guidebook. "It would be a charming place for a rehearsal dinner."

"If the couple was into history," Kate said. "Or trains. Or old mysteries."

"Which they're not," I admitted.

Fern clapped his hands together. "It would be the perfect place to stage Leatrice's murder mystery wedding." He saw me glaring at him, and his shoulders sagged. "If we were still doing that of course."

"We're here for Hailey's wedding," I reminded him as I stood. "Not Leatrice's."

"Do you think they serve afternoon tea?" Fern asked as I followed him down the stairs of the minibus. "After that drive, I'm starved."

I looked pointedly at his Irish coffee. "As long as it's not a champagne tea." I did not want Fern any tipsier than he already was.

"I could go for some tea," Kate said when we'd assembled on the pavement. "I haven't had a bite since breakfast, and I didn't even get to finish that because Annabelle made me come with her to--"

I elbowed her hard and she rubbed her side, but stopped talking. It wasn't common knowledge that we'd snuck into Betty Belle's room, and I wanted to keep it that way.

"Back on the bus in two hours, ladies," Fern called as the older women began to wander off in small groups. He glanced back at the driver and blew him a kiss. "Thanks, Seamus."

The sandy-haired man nodded. "I'll be off to find petrol then."

We watched as the minibus disappeared around the back of the hotel.

"I'd rather tour the property before having tea," I said. "I want to take some photos to send back so we can show our client we're actually working over here."

"Suit yourself," Fern said, extending his arm to Kate. "We'll try to save you some scones."

"I'm with Annabelle." Mack joined us. "I'd like to scout out the ceremony options. Apparently you can get married inside the abbey tower or on the abbey terrace with the abbey as the backdrop."

"There's also a walled garden," Buster said. "In case the bride is too spooked by the body we found in the other one."

"Not that we're going to tell her, right?" I gave Buster and Mack a pointed look. "It isn't lying. It's just not telling her unless she asks."

"So if she asks us, we can tell her the truth?" Mack asked.

"If our bride randomly asks if we found a dead body in the gardens, you have my permission to tell her," I said, feeling relatively confident it was a safe allowance.

"We're going to look at the walled garden," Grace said from behind me.

I hadn't known she and her much quieter husband were behind us, and I jumped at the sound of her voice.

"We'll catch up to you later," Fern said as he pulled Kate with him toward the main building, and the newlyweds started walking hand in hand toward the grounds.

"I forgot they were still here," Richard said once they were out of earshot. "Do we think he speaks?"

"I've had enough groomzillas to be thrilled he isn't chatty," I said as we followed Buster and Mack toward the turreted abbey tower. I paused in front and took a photo with my camera, glad the day had turned sunny, and the gray building stood out against the background of a blue sky.

"If he's actually a groom," Mack said.

"What do you mean?" I asked, almost tripping over my own feet.

"Didn't you notice?" Mack rubbed a hand over his dark-red goatee as he turned to me. "Neither of them are wearing wedding bands."

20

"How could I have missed that?" I said to Richard as we stepped through the heavy wooden doors leading into the abbey.

"What do you mean?" He paused at the back while Buster and Mack strode across the rose-colored carpet toward the arched stained glass windows at the far end of the long room. "You never size up the engagement rings like you should."

He was right. I didn't do the one-glance jewel appraisals he and Fern were capable of doing. "I guess I'm focused on other things. Plus, it seems awkward to stare at someone's diamond during an interview."

"Trust me, darling. You want to spot a cubic zirconia before you get too far along in the process."

I knew in Richard's book, fake diamonds were right up there with fake handbags when it came to crimes against humanity.

"So do you think they aren't really married?" I asked, my voice echoing as I entered the small church.

He tilted his head back to gaze up at the high peaked ceiling crossed with wooden beams. "Who knows? All I know is they seem to have a lot of unplanned time for honeymooners."

"It could be they just aren't wearing nice jewelry because

they're traveling," Buster said, his deep voice reverberating off the ceiling and sounding even louder than usual.

"I never thought about that," I said.

"Because you don't own fine jewelry, darling," Richard said. "Which is another topic for another day."

I thought about telling him I might be the owner of some real jewelry in the not-so-distant future since my boyfriend had mentioned marriage, but even thinking about it made my palms sweaty. I also didn't want to deal with Richard swooning in the middle of the abbey. He hadn't always taken my relationship with Reese in stride.

I walked halfway up the aisle, running my hand across the smooth tops of the wooden chairs arranged in rows of threes. Arched windows on the sides let in natural light, and the stained glass in the main windows was so light it barely cast any color into the room. I expected a building as old as the abbey to be musty, but since the space had been renovated and looked as modern as a new church on the inside, the only scent was that of the floral arrangement on the altar table.

"It's intimate," Mack said as he touched a hand to the pink garden roses in the arrangement.

"That's code for too small, isn't it?" I asked, making a mental calculation of the space. I pulled out my phone and snapped a few photos.

"Unless Hailey wants to cut her guest count," Buster said, flipping open the folder for her wedding.

I shook my head. "We wouldn't even be able to fit her father's colleagues from the Hill in here."

"You really should sell more of your clients on elopements," Richard said. "A ceremony in here would be charming."

I narrowed my eyes at him. "You mean I should talk my clients out of hiring me? Remember, they don't hire me, I can't recommend you."

"Never mind," he said. "You make an excellent point, darling."

Buster joined us in the middle of the room. "I think we can safely cross this space off our list."

I sighed. "I suppose it's good we saw it."

"The Corrib Suite in the other building can hold up to one hundred and seventy guests," Mack said. "It has windows that overlook the estate."

"Look who studied," Richard said.

Mack grinned at him. "Annabelle did send us a ten-page dossier before we left. I assumed there would be a quiz."

I put my hands on my hips. "You know I like to be prepared. And the trip isn't over." I shifted my eyes to Richard. "There still may be a quiz."

"Why don't we check out the Oriental Express Pullman cars next?" Buster suggested. "It's still early enough that they won't be setting up for dinner yet."

We left the abbey and followed the path across the front of the main building and around the side. Our minibus was no longer idling at the base of the sweeping stone staircase that led up to the front door, and I assumed Seamus had found a parking lot in the back. All around the historic house stretched perfectly manicured grass, and as we rounded the gray octagonal section of the buildings, I realized most of the lawn was a huge golf course.

"Does the groom play golf?" Richard asked. "Every castle and historic home here seems to have a golf course."

"We're thinking of taking up golf," Mack said, his leather pants creaking as he walked.

"Really?" I tried not to sound too shocked, but I knew golf clubs were notoriously strict about attire, and I didn't know if my biker friends owned any clothing that wasn't made of cow.

Mack nodded eagerly. "We're excellent at mini golf. How different could it be?"

"Do you see any giant windmills?" Richard said, dodging me as I tried to jab him with my elbow.

"I think you guys would be great," I said. "But do you have

time for a new hobby between your business, your motorcycle club, and the baby?"

"Probably not," Mack said. "We may have to wait until we're retired, although we always envisioned opening a B&B once we hung up our florist shingle for good."

"A B&B?" I didn't even try to suppress the surprise in my voice this time. "I had no idea."

"It's an idea we toss around when the brides are driving us crazy," Buster said. "You know, move out to the country, buy a big old house, renovate it, and open up a B&B."

"Obviously this would be after baby Merry is all grown up." Mack sniffled. "I can't even think of that without crying."

It still surprised me that such tough-looking guys were total marshmallows. I rubbed Mack's arm. "That's still a long way off."

"I think it sounds divine," Richard said. "We all should be planning for life after brides. Let me know if you need someone to be in charge of the breakfast part of your B&B. Annabelle can tell you I make scones to die for."

As we continued on the path down toward the Pullman cars, my mind raced. I'd never given much thought to my life after brides. I'd been going full-force building Wedding Belles for over five years, and it had never occurred to me to think about what I would do afterward. Would there even be an afterward, or would I plan weddings until I dropped? That wasn't an appealing prospect.

Despite what people thought, wedding planning was a physically demanding job, and wedding days required me to be on my feet for over twelve hours. My entire body ached at the end of the night, and it took most of the next day to recover. I doubted I could hack it in another fifteen or twenty years. Or that I'd want to.

"Have you really thought about what you'll do after you give up catering?" I asked Richard.

"Most of the men in my family have died young," he said with a wistful look. "I always assumed I'd be a brilliant flame that burned out far too soon." He let out a huff of breath. "Then a voodoo priestess in New Orleans told me I'd live until ninety and messed up all my plans. Now I have to think about the future. If that lady reading my chicken bones hadn't terrified me, I would have given her a piece of my mind."

I didn't know what to say to that, so I followed him mutely, both pleased he wouldn't die young and disturbed he was putting his faith in a chicken bone prediction. As dismissive as Richard was about Fern's ghost sightings, I knew he did put stock in voodoo, probably because he hailed from near New Orleans. I also knew he was the owner of more than one voodoo doll, and I made it a point to stay on his good side so he wouldn't get one that looked like me.

We rounded the corner and were greeted by two burnished gold lion statues flanking the entrance to the maroon Pullman cars. A pair of black lanterns perched over the arched doorway and hanging baskets of multicolored flowers hung on either side. The hotel had built a patio around the cars that were joined together lengthwise and hedges surrounded one side of the stone platform while garden boxes edged the other.

"It's fun to think one of these cars was used in the filming of the old movie version of *Murder on the Orient Express,*" I said.

"It was also used to carry the remains of Winston Churchill back to his ancestral home for burial," Richard said, reading again from the dog-eared pages of his guidebook.

A shiver went through me as Mack clutched my arm. "Do you think we should go in?"

"It's been totally restored," I said. "People dine here every evening."

Mack bobbed his head up and down but didn't make a move to enter.

I tugged him forward. "I'll snap a few photos; you and Buster can see how you might decorate it, and we'll leave."

Richard tucked his guidebook under his arm and led the way, pulling open the door and holding it for me. It took my eyes a moment to adjust as I stepped inside. The carriage was narrow with lots of dark wood and burgundy upholstery that seemed to suck up the light. Lace curtains hung in the windows, allowing the afternoon sun to slip through, but no lights were on. Crisp white cloths hung over the tables in anticipation of dinner, and vases of flowers mingled with folded napkins and crystal stemware.

"It feels like we stepped back in time," I whispered.

Richard gave a small groan as he took in the setup. "It appears that fan fold napkins will outlast us all."

"I think it looks nice," I said, feeling my shoes sink into the plush burgundy and gold carpet.

Buster scratched some notes in his folder. "It might work for a bachelor party or a small rehearsal dinner, but I don't think it would hold Hailey's numbers."

I scanned the length of the train car and counted the number of bench seats with high upholstered backs. "You're right. We'll have to bring another wedding over here to use it."

"That's the attitude," Mack said.

I gave a final look before turning to go, and my eye caught a flash of something poking out from a banquette at the end. I nudged Richard. "Do you see that?"

He squinted and frowned, walking ahead of me and stopping abruptly when he reached the booth. He staggered back a few steps and made a strangled squeak.

"What is it?" I felt my stomach clench as I approached him and slapped a hand over my mouth when I saw what had caused the color to drain from his face.

It wasn't hard to figure out that the bright-red hair attached to the woman crumpled on the floor belonged to Nancy.

21

"What did I tell you about those Pullman cars?" Fern asked, his voice low and his face stricken as he and Kate huddled together, their arms wrapped around each other.

"At least she wasn't dead," I said, watching Nancy being attended by paramedics in yellow-and-green jackets.

Richard sucked a breath into a paper bag and looked up at me. "She looked dead." He hung over at the waist trying to slow his hyperventilating. It had taken a moment when the paramedics arrived to determine that Richard wasn't the one who needed medical attention. Luckily, Fern had already made a visit to the gift shop and had a paper bag at the ready when he and Kate rushed out of the house to join us.

"Whoever did this left her for dead," Mack said, his eyes not leaving the elderly woman's prone form.

The paramedics had taken Nancy off the Pullman once they'd determined she still had a faint pulse, and she lay stretched out on the paving stones surrounding the train cars. From what I could gather from the conversation between the men working on her, she'd been hit on the head. Although it had knocked her out, the blow hadn't been hard enough to kill her. But who did it? I looked around. No evidence of security cameras pointing toward the train cars. So much for that idea.

I was glad to be out of the stuffy train car and breathing fresh air, even though the sun was beginning to sink lower in the sky, slats of gold light was peeking through the trees, and the temperature was dropping. I rubbed my arms, more to combat the feeling of finding Nancy's body than to ward off the chill.

"Someone clearly wanted to do away with her," Buster said.

"But why?" Kate asked.

That was the million-dollar question, I thought. Why were members of this tour group of seemingly harmless old ladies being targeted?

I watched as Nancy moved her head and her eyes fluttered open. I felt my entire body relax. At least we weren't dealing with another murder scene. Not that a woman being attacked and nearly killed wasn't a big deal, but I didn't relish the idea of leaving a dead body at every wedding venue.

"If I didn't know better, I'd think we were being set up." Richard pulled another breath into the paper bag, then coughed and spluttered, dropping the bag and pulling a five Euro note from his mouth.

Fern giggled and reached for it. "Sorry about that, sweetie. I dropped the change in the bag."

Richard wiped his mouth with the back of his hand and began digging around in his man bag, no doubt for sanitizer. Or new lips.

"What do you mean?" I asked, watching from the corner of my eye as they moved Nancy to a gurney.

Richard produced a small container of hand sanitizer and squirted a liberal amount into his palms. "The killer used Kate's scarf to commit murder and then someone planted Colleen's luggage tag in her room. And now we happen to be the ones to find Nancy on an outing Fern planned? I wouldn't be surprised if a criminal mastermind had plotted this to ruin us."

"Someone's trying to ruin us by killing American retirees?" Kate cocked an eyebrow. "That seems like a stretch. If they wanted to get us, why not just try to murder us?"

Richard's mouth gaped and his eyes darted at the hedges as if a killer might leap out. "Why not indeed?" He passed the sanitizer to me, and I shook my head. He thrust it at me. "We just found a dead body on a train that once carried a dead body. If there has ever been a time to use antibacterials, darling, this is it."

"Let's all calm down a bit." I took the clear plastic container, pouring a few drops of the fast-drying liquid into my hands. "I know this situation isn't great, but I don't think we're in danger."

"Not great?" Richard's voice rose a few octaves. "'Not great' is bandage dresses on women over forty or micro bangs on anyone. *This* is a disaster."

"Nancy?" The shriek made us all turn as the rest of the tour group spilled out of the side of the house.

I didn't know many of the other women by name, but I recognized the woman who'd yelled out as Deb, Myrna's right-hand woman. Myrna was stone-faced beside her.

I stepped forward to intercept the group as they reached the patio. "She's going to be okay. It's only a bump on the head."

Richard made a noise behind me and the ladies glanced over at him, their faces registering confusion.

I took Myrna's arm. "Don't listen to him. He had a bit of a shock when we found her."

"Found her?" Deb craned her neck to watch as the paramedics tightened Nancy's straps on the stretcher. "Where was she?"

"Why wasn't Nancy with the rest of your group?" I asked. "I thought you all went off together from the bus."

"We did." Deb didn't take her eyes off Nancy as she pressed a hand to her throat. "We decided to have tea first, just like your friends." She motioned to Kate and Fern with her head. "We went inside the house, and several ladies went off to the powder room. I assumed she was one of those, although she didn't come back to the restaurant. We saved her a seat, though."

"So after you walked into the house, Nancy disappeared?" I asked.

Myrna cast her eyes to the side. "I think she came into the house with us. I know she was with our group when we started up the stairs from the bus."

"But you can't be sure?" I pressed her, knowing that it was a short walk from the front of the house to the Pullman cars off to the right side.

"I guess I can't," she admitted. "But why would she have been all the way over here?"

"A lot of people come here to see the train," I said. "It's not unusual given its history. Maybe she had the same thought we did and wanted to take a peek before they started to get ready for dinner service."

Deb nodded. "Nancy was more independent than most of us. If anyone would have decided to see the train on her own, it would be her."

"Did anyone else from your group leave during tea or come late?" I asked.

"I don't know," Deb said. "We were at different tables, and I wasn't keeping an eye on what everyone was doing. I do know that not everyone was seated at the same time."

"Because some women were in the bathroom?" I asked.

More nodding from Deb. "Are you sure she's going to be okay?"

"That's what the paramedics said. They're taking her to the hospital though." I watched the woman bite the edge of her thumbnail.

"Why don't I go with her?" Deb said as she wrung her hands.

Myrna squared her shoulders. "I'll join you."

Deb hesitated then nodded. The two women hurried off toward where the other members of their group were falling in step behind Nancy as she was being wheeled to the ambulance in the parking lot.

"I don't know about you," Fern said, "but I'm ready to go."

"Yes, please." Richard shifted his bag on his shoulder. "As pretty as it is, I think I can safely mark Glenlo Abbey off the potential wedding venue short list."

"You're only saying that because we found Nancy nearly dead in the train car," I said.

Fern shuddered. "If we eliminate every venue where we stumble onto bodies, we may not have many options."

"I hope that's not true," I said. "We still have half a dozen venues to check out."

Fern made a face. "We're going to run out of old ladies."

Mack looked horrified, and I patted his thick forearm. "He's not being serious."

Kate looked down at her phone. "It's time to meet back at the bus anyway. I can't wait to get back to my room at the castle and take a hot shower. I'm beat."

"I don't know why you're tired," Richard muttered. "You were eating scones while we were finding the body."

My stomach rumbled at the thought of a scone. So much for having tea after touring the property. I'd been so distracted by finding Nancy and the arrival of the paramedics, I'd forgotten that it was dinnertime.

"I thought we were going to stop at The Cliffs of Moher on the way back." Fern hooked arms with Kate as they led the way down the path to the front of the house.

"You want us to go walk along a sheer drop-off of over seven hundred feet?" Richard asked. "After one person has been killed and another seriously wounded, and we have no idea who's behind it?"

"Oh," Fern said. "I see your point."

"Why not just take us to an armory and be done with it?" Richard threw his arms up. "I, for one, plan to go back to the hotel, cover myself in bubble wrap, and not emerge until the killer has been captured." He took long strides to pass Fern and Kate, leaving us all behind as he barreled toward the minibus.

"Is he serious?" Buster asked.

"He'll get over it," I said. "He always does."

We reached the bus and Buster and Mack lumbered up the steps, causing the vehicle to sway from one side to the other.

I peeked my head inside then looked behind me at Fern. "It looks like everyone is here but the newlyweds and Deb."

"Deb and Myrna went with Nancy," someone reminded me from inside.

"So we're just waiting on Grace and . . ." My words trailed off as I forgot the groom's name.

"Derek." Fern looked around. "I wonder where they went. I know I didn't see them after we all got off the bus."

"Neither did we," I said. "They mentioned the walled garden, but I'm surprised they didn't cross paths with the rest of us at some point. Especially after the ambulance screeched up out front."

"You don't think they're . . ." Fern wagged his eyebrows at me.

"No," Kate shook her head. "They definitely didn't seem like the type."

"The type to do what?" I asked, growing impatient with their veiled comments.

"You know," Fern said, giving me a knowing look that was clearly wasted. "The type to try hanky-panky in public places."

I stared at him. "That's a type?"

"Sure." Kate nodded slowly. "I've dated some guys who--"

I held up a hand to stop her. "I do *not* want to hear the rest of that sentence."

She grinned at me. "Your loss. I'm telling you, those two didn't seem the type."

I usually deferred to Kate's judgment when it came to

anything having to do with men, dating, or hanky-panky. I scanned the grounds and abbey, but saw no one and it was already five minutes past when we were scheduled to leave. "Tell me this then, did they seem the type to try to kill someone?"

22

"You think just because they were late getting back to the bus that we should suspect them of murder?" Fern whispered as we made our way back to our rooms in Dromoland Castle.

"They were only ten minutes late," Kate reminded me, pausing with her hand on her doorknob.

"I'm with Annabelle." Richard bustled past us on his way to his room a few feet down the hallway, the burgundy walls and carpeting seeming darker now that the sun had almost set. "We can account for everyone's whereabouts except for those two."

"Why would a newlywed couple want to whack an old lady over the head?" Fern asked.

"If they're newlyweds at all," I said, giving a nod to Buster and Mack who were a few feet behind us. "They aren't even wearing rings."

Fern fluttered a hand in the air. "Only because Grace discovered she had an allergic reaction to platinum. She explained that to me on the plane."

"Who's allergic to platinum?" Richard said, opening his door with a swipe of his key. "And that doesn't explain the groom's lack of a ring."

"A show of solidarity, I assume," Fern said. "You can't tell me you think they faked those looks of horror when they heard what happened to poor Nancy."

The couple had looked shocked when Fern had told them what they'd missed, but if someone could commit murder, faking surprise would be easy in comparison. Besides, I'd met too many killers who appeared genuinely startled by murders they'd perpetrated.

"As much as I'd love to stand out in the hall and debate who's behind the latest catastrophe," Richard said, "I have a phone call to make."

"We do too," Mack said, looking at Buster. "We promised to Skype with Prue every day so she wouldn't get lonely being with the baby alone."

I knew the real reason probably had less to do with Prue being lonely and more about the men missing baby Merry.

"Kiss the baby for us," Kate said. "There is a hot shower calling my name."

Fern took out his flask and shook it. "And a bottle of Jameson is calling mine. I think I know why the Irish love their whiskey. It's pretty stressful over here."

"I doubt the average citizen of Ireland deals with as many murders and attempted murders on a daily basis as we have," I said. "Their murder rate is actually very low."

Fern pressed a hand to his chest. "You don't think we brought our murder juju with us, do you?"

"We don't have murder juju," I said, hoping if I said it forcefully enough it would be true. "We just have bad luck."

"You keep telling yourself that, darling," Richard said before disappearing into his room.

Everyone else followed suit with waves and promises to get together later for dinner, but I could tell from the weary voices it would take a lot to drag people out again.

I pushed open the door to my room and practically stumbled to the four-poster bed, kicking off my black flats and dropping my black nylon tote bag as I flopped onto the white duvet. The day felt like it had stretched out forever, between sneaking into Betty Belle's room in the morning, to touring the property and getting stuck in the rain under the gazebo, to taking the ill-fated field trip to Glenlo Abbey. I closed my eyes and let my head sink back into the fluffy pillows, breathing deeply. The room service plates from the night before had been cleared away while I was out and the smell of stale food replaced by the faint scent of lemon cleanser. I suspected the hotel maids had also left me a stack of fresh towels and a new assortment of toiletries.

I fought the urge to open my eyes and check as I tried to release the stress of the day and clear my mind of all the questions swirling around inside.

Who had attacked Nancy and why? It had to be connected to Colleen's murder, but how? Were the newlyweds Derek and Grace really who they claimed to be, and why did they happen to turn up where we were staying? There were too many coincidences. I remembered what Reese said: things were connected for a reason. There was no such thing as a coincidence in a murder investigation.

My eyes flew open. I needed to call Reese. He would be able to give me an outsider's view on what was going on. There was no point in trying to hide the latest crime since he already knew about Colleen's murder and wouldn't be shocked to hear there was a second crime. Knowing Reese and my own track record, he was probably counting on it. I also knew he didn't believe for a second that I was trying not to get pulled into the investigation. It was hard to feel indignant about it when deep down I knew he was right.

I reached down and dug into my tote bag until I found my phone. I also found a pack of cookies leftover from the plane and opened them while I hit speed dial.

"Hey, babe," he said when he answered.

"Is this a good time to talk?" I asked, falling back onto the pillows and stretching my feet out in front of me, crossing them at the ankles.

"You know I always like to talk to you," he said. "Hold on a second though."

I took a bite of the brown Biscoff cookie while he clicked over to what I assumed was another caller. I was so hungry, I devoured the entire packet and tossed the cellophane wrapper on the bedside table before Reese returned.

"Sorry about that," he said when he clicked back over. "So is everything okay?"

I let out a breath. "Not really. There was another incident today. Another one of the old ladies was attacked, although this time she wasn't murdered. She was just knocked unconscious."

"That's not good."

"Obviously, the two attacks are connected, but I have no idea how. Neither of the women seemed to have any enemies or reasons someone would want to kill them."

"That you know of," Reese said. "There has to be a reason these women were targeted, even if you don't know it yet. I highly doubt a serial killer is following a group of retirees around Ireland and picking them off one by one."

"Unless it's a pair of serial killers disguised as newlyweds," I said, then gave him the condensed version of how Grace and Derek had ended up with us. "I can't think of a reason why they'd want two old ladies dead either, but they're the only ones who were unaccounted for today."

"It does seem a bit odd that a couple on their honeymoon would want to hang out with your team and a bunch of retired ladies. I can tell you that if we were on our honeymoon, I would want to be as far away from your colleagues as possible."

My pulse quickened. Had he actually given thought to us going on a honeymoon? I swallowed hard and tried to think of a reply that didn't sound panicky.

"Hold on," Reese said with a sigh. "Someone's beeping in."

I exhaled once he'd clicked away. I needed to get a grip.

Talking about honeymoons did not mean we were walking down the aisle tomorrow. I talked about honeymoons all the time with Kate. Usually about the fact that I had no idea where our couples were going, and Kate felt strongly that I should pay more attention to that detail, but the topic never made my heart race. Why did it make me so nervous to hear my boyfriend talk about us on a honeymoon? Was I scared it was all getting too real?

"I'm back," he said after a minute away.

"Are you sure this is a good time?" I asked, thinking maybe I should get off the call before he said anything else to make me panic. "I know it's been crazy with the case you're working on."

"We arrested the author, so I should be able to put the whole thing to bed today."

"That's great," I said, feeling more at ease talking about his job. "I wish I could say the same thing."

"I wish you couldn't," Reese said. "You're not a detective, remember? You're not supposed to be putting cases away. You're supposed to be, well, I actually forgot what you were supposed to be doing over there."

"Checking out wedding venues," I said. "Which I'm still doing, thank you very much. That's why we were at Glenlo Abbey today."

"An abbey that has a train attached to it? Is that normal?"

I started to answer him when something struck me. "How did you know about the train at Glenlo?"

"Didn't you mention finding the second woman in the train car? I'm pretty sure you said it was on a train."

I recognized the sound of someone trying to cover for a slip of the tongue because I'd done it so often with him. "Nope. I didn't say a word about a train."

"Are you sure?"

I slipped off the bed and padded in my bare feet across the room and out into the hall. I walked down to Richard's room and knocked on his door. "Positive."

Richard opened the door, holding his cell phone to his ear. When he saw me, his mouth fell open and the phone slipped a few inches. I snatched it from him and saw on the screen that he was on hold with Reese.

"Why don't you say hi to Richard," I asked Reese. "Oh, wait, you already have."

I thrust my phone at Richard and he took it.

"Good evening, Detective," Richard said, his voice formal until he dropped it and covered the mouthpiece with his hand. "Yep, she looks pretty steamed." He made an indignant noise. "No, I don't think she's just mad at me."

Richard held the phone out to me. "He wants to talk to you."

"I'll bet he does," I said, taking the phone back and pressing it to my ear. "This had better be good."

"He couldn't reach Leatrice, and he called me so I could go check on his dog," Reese said. "He told me about what happened when I was tracking down Leatrice and Hermès. I was on the phone with him when you called in, then he called back when I left him on hold too long."

"Oh," I said, feeling my ire deflate. I'd assumed Richard was calling Reese to spill the beans about the latest crime in case I decided to hold back from my boyfriend, but it made perfect sense that he was obsessively checking on his dog. "So is Hermès okay?"

"Of course," Reese said. "Sidney Allen told me the two of them were on a walk. Leatrice has been spending a lot of time at the dog park trying to catch sleeper spies."

That sounded about right. "I'm sorry I got upset. My nerves are a little frayed."

"Don't worry about it, babe. I'm counting the days until you get back."

"*If* we get back," I said. "All I want to do is keep my head down for the next few days, gather all the information we need for the wedding, and get on that flight out of Dublin."

I turned as Fern strode into the hall in black pants and a

emerald green silk shirt with a black cummerbund. "What on earth . . .?"

He clapped his hands as he saw me standing in the doorway to Richard's room. "Oh, good. There you are. I got us reservations at a nearby pub that has traditional Irish music. We leave in ten minutes."

"I'd better go," I told Reese. "It looks like Fern is about to run off and join Riverdance."

My boyfriend laughed. "That may be the least surprising thing that's happened since you arrived."

23

"This is a traditional Irish pub?" I asked, eyeing the floor-to-ceiling glass exterior with a modern living room grouping of colorful furniture arranged inside like a department store window display.

"I suppose it's technically a gastropub," Fern said as we stepped off the castle shuttle that had transported us from the castle to the nearby Inn at Dromoland--a more casual hotel option on the grounds of Dromoland. "But it has live music tonight, plus I thought it would be nice to get away from all the castles and abbeys and historic manors."

"I think it looks fun," Kate said. "Do you think they actually seat people in the window?"

Richard gave Kate and me a pointed look. "I think you two have spent enough time in windows already, and you're out of your mind if you think *I'm* going to eat dinner in the window. Do I look like a goldfish to you?"

Since his eyes were bugged out and his cheeks sucked in, I hoped Kate would decline to answer.

"I don't care where we sit, as long as they serve us food," Buster said, patting his belly. "We didn't get scones at Glenlo."

"You missed a treat," Fern said. "If we'd known you were

going to be preoccupied by finding another body, we would have snagged some for you."

"Next time we plan on stumbling over an unconscious old lady, we'll let you know ahead of time," I said, fighting the urge to roll my eyes.

Fern patted my arm. "That's all I'm asking."

Richard made no effort to hide his exasperation with an eye roll so dramatic I feared his eyeballs might roll right out of his head and onto the floor. "Oh, for heaven's sake." He strode into Shannigan's Gastropub without a glance behind him, and we all followed.

The inside of the gastropub was as much of a surprise as the outside with a combination of dark wood against modern purple-and-gold patterned upholstery on banquettes and barstools. A sleek cream-colored hearth dominated one wall, and open-backed shelving held a collection of copper cookery and galvanized tin buckets of grass. One dividing wall of double-sided glass shelving displayed crystal glasses and decanters, while a massive chalkboard wall behind a row of banquettes proclaimed their specialties in swirling letters.

I inhaled the scent of beer and grilled meat, and my stomach rumbled. The stress of finding Nancy had done a good job of hiding my hunger, but the savory scents made me realize just how hungry I was.

A waiter led us through the busy restaurant that hummed with the sounds of people talking and a musical ensemble warming up in one corner. We reached a high table with banquette seating on one side and three high barstools on the other. A large painting of a classic Irish pub scene hung over the table with another similar painting beside it. Between the two, they spanned the wall.

"This is perfect," Kate said as she hopped up onto one of the upholstered barstools.

I thanked the waiter as I slid into the banquette and took one of the menus he handed out. Fern and Richard sat on either side of me, and Buster and Mack sat flanking Kate on the other barstools, their girth overflowing the armless stools.

"Isn't this interesting?" Richard said as he scanned the menu. "You don't see Irish lamb tagine in many pubs, now do you?"

"*Gastro*pub," Fern said, leaning over me. "Emphasis on the gastro. Cuisine in Ireland has become very sophisticated in recent years."

Richard raised an eyebrow at the hairdresser, his eyes dropping to the green silk shirt with blousy sleeves. "You don't say?"

Fern bobbed his head up and down, missing Richard's tone. "And locally sourced is very big." He tapped his menu. "Just look at all the local farms they work with."

"Should I be worried he's switching from hair to food?" Richard asked me under his breath.

"Where did you learn all this?" I asked Fern.

"The adorable concierge at the castle," Fern said. "He's been very helpful."

"Does that answer your question?" I whispered to Richard.

"Why don't we try some of the local craft beers?" Fern suggested when the waiter reappeared. "I like the sound of the Friar Weisse and the Chieftain."

"Sure," I said. "I've done my duty to Guinness already. Something lighter would be good."

"Is there Irish wine?" Kate asked, flipping her menu.

Richard wrinkled his nose. "I can't imagine. Have you seen any vineyards as we've been driving?"

"Then I'll just have a cider," Kate said.

"Bulmer's alright for ye?" the waiter asked.

"Whatever you recommend," Kate said, flashing him a smile and some thigh as she crossed her leg.

"Cider sounds good," Mack said.

"I, for one, am glad to be away from all the other Americans," Richard said once the waiter had left with our drink order.

"Be nice," Fern said. "The ladies have been nothing but lovely to us."

"I wouldn't have as much of a problem with them if their bodies didn't keep turning up underfoot." Richard gave a small shudder.

"At least the last one wasn't dead," I said. "Although I suspect the killer thought she was."

Kate put a hand to her throat. "How awful."

"Annabelle's right," Richard said. "Why would you go to the trouble of knocking someone out and almost killing them? No, that old hippie got lucky."

"We were lucky we didn't run into the killer on the train," Mack said, taking a sip of the pint glass of golden cider placed in front of him. "It couldn't have happened more than a few minutes before we arrived."

"Or unlucky," I said. "Whoever it was couldn't have attacked all of us. If we'd gotten to the train earlier, we might have caught them in the act, and we'd know who was terrorizing these poor old ladies."

Buster took a gulp of his cider and shook his head. "We could have stopped it."

It wasn't hard to imagine any killer stopping dead in their tracks at the sight of Buster and Mack.

"Who are our suspects?" Kate asked, holding up her fingers. "Eliminating the six of us, there are all the other women except for Nancy."

"And the ones who didn't come on the outing," Fern said. "Betty Belle stayed at the castle."

Kate took a drink of her cider and dabbed her lip with her napkin. "I don't even know the other women by name."

"There's Deb," Fern said, fluttering two fingers against his chin. "She's the Rubenesque lady who was so upset. The others who came today were Cynthia, Judy, Myrna, and Suzanne. Oh, and Doreen."

I swigged my Chieftain beer, but eyed the pints of cider longingly. I'd never been much of a beer drinker, so I feared the varied Irish brews were lost on me. "Don't forget Grace and Derek."

Fern let out his breath in a huff. "Are we back to this again?"

"They were with us at Glenlo, and no one could verify their whereabouts during the entire time," I said. "If you ask me, that makes them the prime suspects."

"Why would they want to attack Nancy?" Mack asked, leaning his thick forearms on the table. "And they weren't even at Dromoland when Colleen was killed."

I held up a finger. "We don't know that. Fern saw them at breakfast the next morning. They could easily have checked in before we did the day prior."

"But why would they want to kill either woman?" Buster asked, finishing off his cider and leaning back.

"That I don't know," I admitted. "What we're missing in this case is motive."

"Are you now?"

The voice from behind made us all look up or turn. Garda Ryan stood behind the table with his arms crossed and the corner of his mouth quirked up. He wasn't in his uniform, but wore jeans with a dark sweater.

Kate nearly slipped off her stool. "What are you doing here?"

He caught her before she hit the floor and helped her back into her seat. "Grabbing a pint with some mates."

"You always drink here?" I asked, my eyes scanning the upscale pub for other officers in plain clothes, but I didn't recognize any.

He shrugged. "It's close to where I've been working lately. And the chips are good."

His mention of the chips reminded me we hadn't ordered, and I was still hungry.

"I thought I'd come over and let you know that you're free to leave the area," the handsome garda said. "I know you're here on some sort of business and are eager to be moving along."

"You've got that right," Richard muttered.

"So Kate's no longer a suspect?" I asked.

He shook his head, his eyes darting to Kate and away again after momentarily lingering on her bare leg. "Between all the interviews with guests and staff and the time stamps on her phone photos, we were able to determine she had an alibi for the time leading up to the woman's death."

"And I proved that the evidence against her was circumstantial?" I asked.

He tilted his head at me. "Are you sure you're a wedding planner?"

"She is," Fern said, winking at him, "but she gets that question a lot. She's practically engaged to a police detective back home if that explains anything."

"I'm not engaged," I said, feeling my face warm. "Not yet at least."

Richard's head snapped toward me, but I refused to look at him as my cheeks burned.

Garda Ryan nodded. "It does actually. Does your fiancé involve you in his cases?"

"He's not my fiancé," I insisted, "and he really tries not to."

Mack laughed. "But that doesn't always work. She manages to get in the middle of things anyway."

"Hey," I said. "You know I only get involved if one of us is in danger."

"Or their business is threatened," Richard added. "Like mine was a few months ago."

"Or if she thinks someone has been wrongly accused," Kate said. "Remember Georgia?"

Everyone nodded, and Garda Ryan's eyebrows disappeared beneath his bangs.

"So you were saying we're free to go?" I tried to steer the conversation away from my habit of getting mixed up in investigations. "That's great. Now we just need to find a way to get us all to the next venue."

"Be right back," Richard said, slipping out of the banquette.

I hoped he wasn't upset about all the fiancé talk. Richard hadn't had the easiest time adapting to my relationship with Reese, and I wasn't sure if he was ready for the next step. Or if I was.

"We could always take the train," Fern suggested.

"No trains," Buster and Mack said in unison.

"Oh, right," Fern said.

"So if Kate's not a suspect, do you have any other leads?" I asked the amused guard.

He hesitated. "To be honest with yeh, the case has gone a bit arseways."

"I'm guessing that's not good," I said.

"Too bad we have to leave," Kate said, her voice wistful. "We could help you solve it."

Garda Ryan laughed. "You Americans aren't dull, I'll give ye that."

"Connor! How's the craic?" A man yelled from the bar and the garda raised a hand in acknowledgement.

"Well, that's me off then," he said, giving us a final nod. "Try to stay outta trouble, will ye?"

I shook my head at Kate as we watched the man weave his way through the restaurant to the bar. "I for one am happy to leave the castle where we found a lady floating dead in the garden pond."

"Am I glad we missed that," Mack said, his arms folded across his chest and his eyes almost closed.

I looked at Buster, who also looked more bleary-eyed than when we'd arrived and was slumping on one elbow propped on the table. Then I sized up their empty glasses. Reaching across the table, I grabbed Kate's glass of cider and took a sip. "This is alcoholic!"

"Of course it is," Kate said. "It's Irish cider. What did you expect?"

One of Mack's eyes opened. "It's what?"

"Well, I'm guessing they thought it was like regular old

American apple cider," I said, giving Kate a pointed look. "You know, since they don't drink."

Buster hiccupped. "Are you saying . . .?"

Fern gasped as his eyes slid from one burly man to the other. "They're drunk."

Kate lifted one of the empty pint glasses. "Off one drink?"

"If you haven't had a drop of alcohol in years, sure," I said, rubbing my forehead. "Less than forty-eight hours in Ireland, and we get two teetotalers drunk."

"Is there anything more Irish than that?" Kate asked.

"How about an Irish jig?" Fern said, nudging me to let him out of the banquette as the sounds of traditional Irish music filled the air. "I've been dying to try my hand at Irish dancing."

I stumbled as I let Fern out, watching as he began flailing his feet and hopping around with his hands on his hips.

"I don't feel so good," Mack said, squinting at Fern's spinning figure. "I'm seeing leprechauns."

Kate patted his arm. "That's just Fern, but it's an easy mistake to make."

Richard returned with a triumphant look on his face. "Good news. Seamus was able to hook me up with his friend, who also drives minibuses for tourists. I have us booked to leave the first thing in the morning."

"Seamus?" I asked, having to raise my voice over the music.

"The Irishman who's driving the old ladies. The one who drove us to Glenlo today," Richard said, then took in Kate's dejected face and Buster and Mack slumped over the table. "I thought I'd get a better reaction than this."

"She's upset to be leaving the cute cop," I said, nodding to Kate. "And Buster and Mack are drunk."

Richard opened and closed his mouth a few times.

"You can't say Fern's not excited," I told him as Fern spun near us, one arm waving above his head.

Richard glanced down at his cell phone. "Maybe it's not too late to make our bus a two-seater."

24

"What a glorious morning," Richard said as he came out of Dromoland Castle and slipped his designer sunglasses over his eyes.

"You're just saying that because the bus is here and we're leaving the genealogy tour group behind." I dropped my black nylon carry-on bag near the pile of our luggage that was to be loaded into a white Mercedes-Benz Sprinter van.

The morning was cool and crisp, and I was glad I'd thrown on a black cardigan over my button-down shirt. I looked across the parking area to the wet grass and suspected it had rained during the night. The air held the scent of rain, and I hoped that didn't mean we'd be driving through it. I peered up at the clouds. So far the puffs of white in the sky didn't look menacing, but I knew Irish weather could change quickly.

"There are no flies on you, Annabelle." Richard eyed the other shuttle bus and the larger pile of luggage being loaded onto it. "I'm taking it the old ladies got the go-ahead to continue their trip as well?"

"They're off to visit Cork and Cobh," Fern said, joining us outside the castle in a cream-colored fisherman's sweater over brown flannel pants. "Apparently, Cobh was a departure point for ships coming to America and Canada, so it's a good place to look for family names."

"How is it you always seem to be in the know?" I asked. "Did you snag one of their itineraries?"

"I ran into Betty Belle in the lobby," Fern said. "She's so eager to leave this place behind she barely did her hair this morning, the poor dear."

I'd never seen Betty Belle's snowy bouffant anything but pristine, so I knew the stress of Colleen's murder and Nancy's attack must be getting to her. "What about Nancy? Is she joining them or flying back to the U.S.?"

Fern waved a hand. "Apparently she's flying home. She refused to stay in the hospital because she claimed it had bad energy, so the doctors let her go."

"That seems a bit soon," Richard said.

"All she had was a mild concussion." Fern dropped his Louis Vuitton duffel bag on top of a hard-sided suitcase. "These old birds are tougher than they look."

I nudged him as a few of the ladies emerged from the castle. He may get away with calling our brides back home "floozies" and "tramps," but I doubted if he could get away with affectionate insults with these ladies.

"Too bad she claims not to remember a thing about being attacked," I said, wishing I'd been able to question her myself instead of relying on hearing it secondhand from Fern who heard it from Betty Belle who heard it from Deb.

Richard shrugged. "Not a shock since she was hit on the back of the head."

I knew he was right, but it still left me frustrated with no more information about the attacker than before.

"Has anyone seen Kate this morning?" I asked, looking for her blond head over the sea of gray ones.

"She was on her cell in the lobby," Fern said. "It sounded like she was setting up goat yoga for a bride, but I could be mistaken. It is still early."

"No, that sounds right." I sighed. "One of our June brides wants to do goat yoga with her bridesmaids the morning of the wedding."

Richard made a face. "Goat yoga?"

"You know," I said. "You do yoga while cute baby goats climb all over you."

"And I would want to do this why?" Richard looked horrified. "Who knows where those hooves have been?"

I spotted Buster and Mack lumbering down the stone steps. Even though they'd only had one pint of alcoholic cider the night before, I also knew they never drank, so the booze had hit them hard. It had taken significant effort to wake them up and drag them from the gastropub, and Mack had been snoring before his head hit the pillow in his room.

"How are you two feeling?" I asked when they reached us.

"Good." Mack stroked his goatee. "I slept like a log."

"It must have been the jet lag," Buster said, "because I haven't slept that soundly in ages."

"Probably because we aren't listening for the baby's cries." Mack snapped his fingers. "We watch Merry overnight sometimes, and we never get good sleep when we're listening for her cries."

"That must be it," Richard said, his voice tinged with sarcasm. "It couldn't have been the pints of--"

I jabbed him with my elbow. If they didn't remember drinking, then we weren't going to be the ones to remind them they'd accidentally imbibed.

"Is this our van?" Buster asked, climbing in the open door as the van lurched to one side from his weight. He peered in and then leaned back out. "It's nice."

"You had to get a Mercedes van?" I asked Richard but not loud enough for anyone else to overhear.

"Yes, I did," he said. "There's no reason why we should suffer. We already had to fly coach."

"You driving?" Buster asked as he looked at the empty driver's seat.

"Not on your life. The driver popped inside for a cup of tea," Richard said. "As soon as he comes back out and Kate joins us, we can be off."

"I'd better say my goodbyes to the ladies." Fern produced a monogrammed handkerchief from a pocket. "I hope there aren't waterworks."

Richard shook his head as Fern hurried off. "We've only known them for a few days."

"You know how attached he gets," I said. "He cries at the end of every wedding even though most of the brides end up coming back to him to get their hair done."

"As far as I'm concerned," Richard said, "the end of the wedding is the best part. I've been paid. The client is happy. I don't have to talk to them again."

"They don't call you after the wedding to catch up?" I asked, having fielded two of those "catch up" phone calls the week before.

"Catch up?" He pressed a hand to his chest. "About what? Annabelle, we are not their friends. We're the hired help. As close as you think you get to them and as much personal dirt as you know about their families, you are not their friends."

"I know," I said, pulling my hair up into its usual ponytail. "But after talking to some of them every day for over a year, it's hard for them to go cold turkey. I usually wean them off with a few phone calls."

Richard gave a sharp shake of his head. "Not me. At the end of the reception, we are broken up. Unless you have an upcoming party or you get knocked up on the honeymoon and need a caterer for the baby shower, do not keep calling me."

I rolled my eyes at him. "I know you're not as tough as you pretend to be. You like your clients. What about last year when you walked around saying you loved your clients for months."

"That's because I was trying affirmations," he said with a sniff. "They didn't work."

I watched Fern blow his nose loudly as he hugged a horrified Myrna. "There has to be a happy medium."

"Let me know when you find it," Richard said. "Along with life-work balance and decent sugar-free anything."

I saw Kate running down the stairs, her black Longchamp bag bouncing on her hip, and her high-heeled green mules clomping on the stone steps. "Looks like we can get on the road."

"We have a problem," Kate said when she reached me.

"With goat yoga?"

She shook her head. "With the driver. He just got violently ill inside."

"What driver?" Richard asked. "Seamus?"

"No," I said, pointing to the sandy-haired man loading the ladies' luggage into their bus. "He's right here."

"The driver for our bus," Kate said. "At least he said he was our driver when they asked him who he was inside the castle."

I felt my stomach sink. "Our driver is sick?"

Richard sucked in his breath. "Impossible. He looked fine when he arrived. He said he was going to get a cup of tea before we left."

Kate held up her hands. "I'm just saying what I saw." She grimaced. "And it wasn't pretty. If you ask me, he was nursing a hangover that wasn't quite over. No way is he going to be able to drive. He could barely stand upright without retching."

Richard staggered back a few steps. "This trip is cursed."

"It's not cursed," I said, motioning for him to be quiet as some of the ladies began glancing our way. "We've had a few hiccups is all."

"Hiccups?" Richard's voice became shrill. "A hiccup is losing your luggage, not finding bodies every time you turn around and having drivers struck down by mysterious illnesses."

A lady in a pink "Fur Grandma" sweatshirt gaped at Richard

as he began fanning himself with both hands and walking in a circle muttering to himself.

"It hasn't been every time we turn around," I said. "To be fair, we've only found one dead body so far."

Kate nodded. "Which is under par for us if you think about it."

"That's right," Mack said. "The second lady was only knocked unconscious."

"And if the driver is hungover, that isn't exactly a mysterious illness," Kate said.

"Are you people insane?" Richard stopped and stared at us, then waved a hand at the nearby women. "Those old ladies are dropping like flies, and we've spent half our trip being interrogated by the local police."

I smiled at the ladies who were now clutching each other with wide eyes. "He didn't mean that. It's been a long few days, and he's away from his dog."

The lady in the "Fur Grandma" sweatshirt nodded, but the rest did not look comforted by my explanation.

"What's going on?" Fern asked, joining us as he dabbed his eyes.

"We're down a driver," Kate told him.

"And up a nervous breakdown," I muttered.

Fern's eyes lit up. "Does that mean we need to share a bus with the ladies again?"

"No," Richard said a little too loudly. "We're going in entirely different directions. We have to be at Ballyfin Demesne by this afternoon come hell or high water."

Fern glanced up as a raindrop hit him on the forehead. "Well, I think you may have to go with high water because the skies look like they're about to open up."

I followed his gaze to the dark cloud that had moved in above us. "So what do we do? Call for a backup driver?"

Kate waved a hand at the white van. "We have the vehicle. We just need someone to drive it."

"Don't even think about it," I said.

Kate backed away. "Calm down. I wasn't suggesting me, but there must be someone else in our group who can drive a stick shift."

"I can," Buster leaned his head out from the open door of the van. "All our floral delivery vans are manual transmission."

I hesitated. "Are you sure we can just drive off without the driver?"

"What's our alternative?" Kate asked. "Wait until the driver recovers and miss our appointment at the next venue?" She dropped her voice. "Go off to Cork with the old ladies and hunt down our ancestors?"

"When you put it like that," I said.

"Listen," she said, turning toward the castle, "I'll run inside and tell the driver while you guys fire up the engine."

Richard grabbed his wheeled suitcase and began pulling it toward the back of the van where the milk-truck doors stood open. "Frankly, I'd rather take my chances with Buster's driving than have to listen to Fern and those ladies sing show tunes again." He heaved his suitcase into the van. "Come to think of it, I'd take my chances with Kate's driving over that."

"I'm going to pretend I didn't hear you," Fern said as he picked up his Louis Vuitton duffel and headed up the stairs into the van, looking over his shoulder and sighing. "I guess the newlyweds are sleeping in. Too bad we can't say goodbye to them."

Kate ran back out, her face flushed pink. "Done. The poor driver was so sick, I don't think he cared."

I looked up at the gray castle as clouds massed behind it. "I guess it's settled."

Richard adjusted his leather man bag across his shoulder and walked up the stairs behind Fern, pulling out his guidebook. "I should discuss the most scenic route with Buster before he just drives off willy-nilly."

"Just what Buster always wanted," Kate said, rolling her eyes. "Richard as a backseat driver."

Mack helped with the rest of the bags, slamming the back doors shut. "That's everything."

I followed Kate up the stairs and took the black leather seat next to Richard in the front. Buster sat in the driver's seat, his bulk overflowing the chair and one thick arm resting out the open window. Richard was holding out his guidebook and showing him a map, but Buster seemed to be doing a good job of ignoring him.

"Here goes nothing," he said, starting the van.

Fern waved wildly even though the windows were tinted, and I saw several of the sweatshirt clad ladies wave as we drove away. Fat raindrops splatted on the windshield as Buster switched gears and the van lurched forward. He located the windshield wipers as we accelerated down the long drive and the rain pelted the windows. I looked back at the silhouette of Dromoland Castle through the gray mist.

Was someone running after us? I shook my head and the figure seemed to disappear in the rain. Even though I didn't believe our trip was cursed, I felt glad to be putting the castle in the rearview mirror in more ways than one.

25

"It's official," Kate said as she clopped down the steps of the van in her heels. "I'm castled out."

I already stood outside the vehicle looking up at the stone edifice of Ballyfin Demesne, a lavish Regency mansion fronted by pale gray columns and tall windows. "Then you're in luck. This isn't a castle."

Kate shielded her eyes from the sun peeking through the clouds. "It may not have turrets, but it took us ten minutes to drive through the grounds and past the lake. This is no normal historical house."

I'd give her that. Compared to the Federal-style homes we were used to in Washington, DC, this estate was massive with an arched columned portico to one side and stone sphinxes flanking the entrance. I inhaled the scent of freshly mowed grass, no surprise since the estate was surrounded by acres of lush green. Luckily, we seemed to have escaped the rain that had followed us for most of the drive, and the skies about Ballyfin were blue and dotted with only a few diaphanous clouds.

"It's the most notable example of nineteenth-century neoclassical architecture in Ireland," Richard said, reading from his guidebook as he disembarked. "The glass conservatory was added later and can be accessed through a concealed door in a bookcase in the library."

"How delightful," Fern said from behind him. "There were no hidden doors at the last two castles."

On our way to the luxury mansion, we'd stopped at Lisheen Castle and Castle Durrow, both only short detours off our route. One had been a traditional castle with weathered stone and multiple turrets, while the other had been more of a country house hotel with extensive formal gardens. I'd taken lots of pictures at both venues, although my gut told me they weren't what our bride was looking for.

"Castle Durrow didn't look as much like a castle as Lisheen," Kate said. "No turrets or tower, although the gardens were spectacular."

"Agreed," Mack said, lumbering out of the van and stretching his beefy arms overhead. "A ceremony in the gardens at Castle Durrow would be gorgeous."

"Prettier than Dromoland?" I asked.

"Fewer dead bodies than at Dromoland," Richard muttered, closing his guide and slipping it into his black crossbody bag.

"We shouldn't let the murder--and attempted murder--affect our opinion of the venues," I said. "We need to give Hailey our unbiased thoughts on which venue would be best for her wedding. Not which ones had a lower body count."

"Even without the body, I think I like this better," Kate said, eyeing the portico with the neoclassical pediment above soaring columns. "It's a bit flashier."

"I don't care what it looks like at this point," Buster said, coming down the stairs and massaging his hands. "After driving through the rain on the left side of the world's tiniest roads, all I want to do is check in and collapse."

I patted him on the back. "You did an amazing job."

"What about me?" Richard asked. "I navigated."

I wasn't sure if screeching directions from behind the driver was considered navigating, but I patted his arm as well. "You were both brilliant."

A pair of young men in tan vests and turquoise ties emerged from the house.

"We're checking in," Richard said, then glanced back at me. "I'll go get our keys."

I picked up my tote bag as the bellmen began unloading our suitcases from the back of the van. I didn't see bell carts, but since there were two sets of stone steps leading to the entrance, I suspected the men would be carrying our bags in by hand. I dug in my bag for some Euros since they'd need to be tipped well for their effort.

Kate walked apart from us and took a few photos on her phone. "These are for Instagram. I've been posting from every venue."

I felt like smacking myself in the head. Between sending information to Hailey and dealing with the murder investigation, I'd completely forgotten about social media. Not that I minded forgetting. I felt the same way about hashtags that Richard felt about vegan bacon--I could go a lifetime without seeing them again.

"Thanks for remembering," I said. "I haven't been in a very Instagram frame of mind lately."

Kate cocked an eyebrow at me. "Are you ever?"

Fair point. I just didn't feel like everything that happened in life needed to be posted. Luckily, Kate was younger than me and had no problem taking up my social media slack.

She held her phone up high and started talking into it, clearly taking a selfie video. "Hey, it's your girl Kate and I'm at Ballyfin Demesne in Ireland." She pivoted to get me in the shot. "Say hi, Annabelle."

I waved awkwardly at the phone. "Hey, everyone."

Kate clicked off the video and tapped the screen a few times. "There, we posted a story."

Richard poked his body half out of the high wooden doors and waved us in. "I've got our keys."

I glanced around and realized Kate and I were the only ones left standing outside. I hurried inside, my eyes adjusting as I stepped into a pretty entry hall with a marble checkerboard and mosaic-patterned floor and a massive set of antlers mounted to one side. The walls were a muted shade of pumpkin and broken up by square black granite columns that were set flat against the walls. Through a door to the right was a lovely parlor decorated with a green velvet settee and a fringed ottoman in front of an ornate white mantle.

Buster lay sprawled across the settee, and Mack sat across from him in an ivory wingback chair. Both men seemed to dwarf the furniture.

"Ready to go to your room?" I asked.

"Once my legs work normally again," Buster said, not opening his eyes. "I feel like I rode the brakes for the past three hours."

Fern stood at a wooden desk with his Louis Vuitton duffel on one of the upholstered chairs. "I must say, this is quite charming."

I glanced at Fern's bag and then at the identical duffel bag the bellman was walking inside. "Do you have two Louis Vuitton bags or am I starting to see things?"

Fern's head snapped up. "Another Louis?"

Kate lifted the second bag as it was set down in the entryway. "Looks like it. This isn't yours? Or Richard's?"

Richard squinted at the bag and made a face. "It's not mine. You know I don't believe in knockoff bags."

"This is a knockoff?" Kate lifted the dark brown bag with interlocked "Ls" and "Vs" covering the exterior.

Fern waved us into the parlor, and Kate walked the duffel bag in and set it on top of the desk. Richard and I followed.

Fern examined the bag for a moment. "Richard's right. This is no Louis."

"It's a Louie," Richard said. "With an 'ie' instead of a 'uis.'"

Fern swatted at him. "You're so bad." His face became serious again. "All joking aside, you can tell it's a fake because the design doesn't mirror itself at the edges."

I squinted at the fleur-de-lis he pointed at. "You mean because it's cut off at the other end of the bag?"

"Exactly," Fern said, touching the zipper. "And the hardware is too bright a gold. Real Louis Vuitton bags have brass hardware that oxidizes over time."

I studied the shiny gold zipper and then looked at the duller zipper on Fern's duffel bag. "Okay, so this bag isn't yours and it isn't real. That doesn't tell us whose it is and why we have it with us."

Kate slapped a hand to her mouth. "It must be one of the ladies' from the genealogy tour. We were loading up at the same time they were this morning. We left so quickly, we must have grabbed an extra Louis."

"I think that's my fault," Mack said, standing and joining us. "I saw it near our pile and tossed it into the back because I thought it was Fern's."

Fern's eyes grew wide. "I hope it isn't someone's essentials."

"We should probably try to contact them," I said. "Where were they headed again? Cork?"

Fern nodded. "I don't know the name of their hotel though."

"It can't be hard to track down a bus full of American ladies in cat sweatshirts," Richard said. "I'd hope there aren't multiples."

"You want to call every hotel in Cork?" I asked, hearing the weariness in my voice.

"We don't even know for sure whose bag this is," Kate said. "You were buddy-buddy with them. Do you remember which lady had a Louis bag?"

Fern crossed his arms over his chest. "I didn't help them unpack, sweetie."

"Well, it wasn't Betty Belle," I said, remembering the luggage that had been in her room when we'd snuck in.

"That's right." Kate snapped her fingers. "She had one of those Vera Bradley bags."

"Look who has the eagle eyes," Fern looked from me to Kate. "I don't know why you're asking me if you remember so well."

Richard narrowed his eyes at me, and I knew he remembered how we both remembered Betty Belle's luggage so clearly. "This is absurd." He grabbed the fake bag. "All we have to do is open it."

I thought about protesting, and then realized I wasn't one to talk. Richard unzipped the bag and we all looked inside.

"That's odd," Fern said, pulling out a rolled up tea towel.

"It is odd," Richard said. "I thought you bought up all the tea towels in the country."

Fern gave him an arch look as a tarnished metal circle with a pin across it fell out of the tea towel and onto the desk.

"It looks like your brooch pin," I said, picking up the bronze piece, “but a lot older."

Richard reached in and took out another tea towel. This time an ornate bronze bell rolled out, and Kate caught it before it hit the floor.

"I haven't seen one of these in the gift shops." Fern touched the metal chain that wound around the bell. "I would've gotten one."

I felt a knot form in my stomach as I remembered seeing it inside Colleen’s bag when we’d opened it in her room. "I don't think these are things you can buy in a gift shop."

Richard's face looked pale as he met my eyes. "Annabelle is right. These look like artifacts."

"Why would one of the old ladies have a bag filled with Irish artifacts?" Fern asked, pulling more rolled up tea towels and displaying more tarnished and ancient-looking items.

"Because she stole them," I said, my voice dropping to a whisper.

Fern pressed a hand to his throat. "Do you think that's why Colleen was murdered and Nancy attacked?"

"It must be," Kate said. "Maybe they both figured out what was going on."

"What *is* going on?" Fern asked, his face horror-stricken. "You don't think those ladies are running a smuggling ring, do you? They all look so sweet."

"Grandmas in cheesy sweatshirts?" Buster adjusted his goggles from where he sat on the settee. "It would be the perfect cover."

"Have we been driving all over the country with a bag filled with stolen goods?" Richard asked, his voice rising. "Are we now aiding and abetting a criminal conspiracy?" He swung his head to Fern. "I told you those old ladies were trouble, but did anyone listen to me?"

Fern shook his head vigorously, and his low ponytail swung from side to side. "Maybe there's one bad apple, but the whole group? I can't believe it."

"Fern could be right," Mack said. "It would make sense that it's one person trying to keep her illegal actions hidden. That would explain Colleen and Nancy as well. Maybe they were going to blow the whistle."

"You all can't admit a bunch of sweet old ladies could be part of a criminal ring," Richard said, his breathing rapid. "And now we're part of it." He clutched the edge of the table. "We're international smugglers."

I shushed him, looking behind me to make sure the bellmen hadn't heard his mini meltdown. "We are not international smugglers. We took the bag by accident." I began stuffing everything back inside. "And we need to keep this hush-hush."

"We've already been under suspicion for murder," Richard said. "You really think the Gardaí will believe we weren't in cahoots with the other Americans? Thanks to Fern, we were practically bunking with them."

Fern gave him a cutting look. "Well, excuse me for trying to be friendly. I still don't believe all the women were in on it. Some of those dears couldn't keep a secret like that to save their lives." He shook his head. "They were quite the gossips.

Bold words considering most of the juiciest gossip in DC got its start right in Fern's Georgetown salon.

"Either way," I said, zipping up the bag, "we won't know who the mastermind is unless we can figure out whose bag this is."

"Before she figures out we have it and comes after us," Kate said.

Fern gave a small squeak.

I narrowed my eyes at him. "Which is a distinct possibility because you told them exactly where we were going, didn't you?"

He looked at the bag then back at me before his eyes rolled back in his head and he collapsed in a heap, Mack catching him before he hit the carpet.

"I'll take that as a yes," I said.

Richard eyed the limp Fern. "Some people are so dramatic."

26

"So let me get this straight," Reese said, not even attempting to hide the disbelief dripping from his voice. "You accidentally took someone else's fancy bag and it ended up being filled with what you think are stolen artifacts?"

"The key word in all this is 'accidentally,'" I said, holding the phone to my ear as I stood in the glass conservatory attached to the side of the house.

I'd wandered away from the parlor to talk to Reese, and my wanderings had led me to the house's massive library and through the secret door behind a bookshelf. The glass conservatory looked like a giant birdcage with a spectacular view of the grounds. I quickly assessed that it would be perfect for a small ceremony or bridesmaids' luncheon.

"Babe," Reese said, his deep sigh crystal clear despite the thousands of miles between us. "You accidentally get involved in more crimes than some career criminals I know."

"You don't think I wanted the trip to end up this way, do you?" I felt tears prick the backs of my eyes. I'd left Kate to watch over a guilt-stricken Fern while Richard had rushed off to see if he could get us into our Dublin hotel early. None of us relished the thought of waiting until the owner of the bag showed up to claim it, especially since we'd seen what had happened to Colleen and Nancy. Clearly, the thief felt the stolen goods were worth killing over, and now that we'd seen the artifacts, any one of us could be the next victim. "I'm supposed to be here finding a wedding venue, not evading a murderer."

"I'm sorry," my boyfriend said. "I know this isn't your fault, but I think Richard's right. The sweet old ladies aren't all so sweet."

I walked toward one of the two neoclassical statues on each end of the conservatory and admired the carved drapery. "Wait a second. When did you talk to Richard?"

There was silence from him on the other end, although it sounded like he was walking through a crowd of people. "The other night when he beeped in while we were talking, remember?"

"And he told you his suspicions about the genealogy tour group?"

"You know Richard," he said. "He loves to complain."

That was true. I lifted a hand to shield my eyes from the sun as I gazed at the stair-step water cascade outside the conservatory. It began at the top of a hill under a marble columned portico and stretched down a long verdant lawn to spill into a pool with a lounging stone figure I assumed to be a Roman god. Talk about an impressive view.

"He also asked me to look into some of the women," Reese continued. "Along with the newlyweds who were tagging along."

"Richard asked you to do background for him?" I felt my mouth dropping open. "I thought you weren't allowed to run checks on people if it wasn't related to your cases?"

"I'm not, but Richard made it seem like it was life or death over there."

I turned and walked to the celadon-green wicker furniture grouped in the center of the room and flopped down against the green-and-white floral cushions. "Well, for once his drama may not have been exaggerated."

"Don't let him hear you say that."

"Never," I said, allowing myself a small smile. "So what did you find out?"

Muffled voices in the background made him raise his voice. "Not much. The newlyweds were a dead end, although I'm not sure I had enough information to do a decent search since I didn't know where they're from."

"Richard will be disappointed," I said. "He's not a big fan of those two."

"Then he's not going to be happy about the rest either. Aside from some personal scandal, none of the ladies have a criminal record. At least the ones Richard got full names for."

I sat up. "Scandal? What kind of scandal?"

"A couple of your women are widows a few times over, including one who's had three husbands die of heart attacks, each one leaving her wealthier than before."

I felt a flutter of excitement. "Were any of the heart attacks suspicious?"

"No," Reese said. "Should I be disturbed that your voice perked up at the mention of dead husbands?"

My cheeks warmed. "My voice didn't perk up. It's just interesting. Who has all the dead husbands? Betty Belle?"

More loud voices in the background. Georgetown must be hopping, I thought, knowing how crowded the sidewalks could get sometimes, especially when the weather was nice.

"Someone named Myrna Rooney," he said over the cacophony.

"Myrna?" I nearly slipped off the rattan armchair. "The steely-haired battle-ax has romanced more than one man?"

"According to the records," Reese said, "she's pretty well off at this point."

I thought for a moment. "That explains how she can travel to Ireland every year, but it also eliminates her motive for stealing the artifacts. If she's rich, why would she go to the trouble?"

"Did you think Myrna was behind the attacks in the first place?" Reese asked.

I shook my head even though he couldn't see me. "Not really. I mean, she's not exactly warm and fuzzy, but I also don't think she'd ruin her own trip like this."

"So she's not the type of woman you'd want to marry, but she probably isn't your killer."

I leaned back in the chair and took a deep breath. "You said more than one of the women had been widowed more than once. Who else?"

"Colleen, the first victim. She had two husbands and both died, but they didn't leave her wealthy. Actually, she was almost bankrupt when she died."

"That's interesting," I said. "Fern gave me the impression that all the women on the trip were well-off."

"Don't take Fern's word as gospel. Only about half of the women Richard told me about are wealthy."

I remembered Betty Bell making a catty comment about Deb having no money and Colleen bristling at it. Now it made more sense. "Well, even if poor Colleen desperately needed the money, she can't be the smuggler because she's dead."

"That does make her a long-shot suspect," Reese said.

Talking over the potential suspects with my boyfriend had calmed me down a bit, and the peaceful setting hadn't hurt. "Thanks for talking me off the ledge."

"That's what I'm here for," he said, "although I really wish you were here instead of there. I don't like the idea of you and your band of cohorts gallivanting around Ireland with a killer on your trail."

"That makes two of us," I said, rubbing a hand across my forehead. "I'm ready to come home and not leave our apartment for a week."

"Sounds perfect." His voice got husky. "We can tell Leatrice we're going away, then turn off all the lights and not leave the bedroom."

I couldn't think of what to say as I fanned my face with the nearest cushion. Part of me was ready to dump the bag of artifacts at the door of the nearest Gardaí station and head for the airport. We'd gathered enough information about wedding venues, hadn't we? As I looked over the stunning grounds and made a mental checklist of all the amazing photo ops, something told me that Hailey would end up getting married here.

"No, you can't get married there," Kate said into her phone as she walked into the conservatory behind me. "The National Zoo does host weddings, but not *inside* the animal enclosures."

I raised an eyebrow at her, and she gave me an eye roll that confirmed she was talking to one of our newest clients. Kate was a master of using tough love when it came to narrowing venues for couples. It always astounded me where people wanted to get married and that they couldn't comprehend why it wouldn't work. Only a bride would think it was reasonable to risk being mauled for her wedding.

"What about the Museum of Natural History?" Kate suggested as she paced the length of the glassed space. "They only recently started allowing wedding receptions. Your guests could eat dinner around the giant elephant."

"Is that Kate I hear?" Reese asked.

"Yep. She's talking with one of our new clients." I let out a breath. "That's one thing I'm not looking forward to when we get back. Tons of catch-up meetings."

"So my idea of hibernating in our bedroom . . .?"

"May not be completely practical," I said. "But things get slower in late July and early August. Almost no one gets married then."

"Except wedding planners, right?"

My throat went dry.

"Didn't you tell me once that wedding planners and other people in the wedding business plan their own weddings for the off-season?"

"I told you that?" I asked, hearing the crack in my voice. "And you remembered it?"

"Of course I remembered."

"Why do I seem to spend half of my life tracking you down?" Richard asked as he burst into the room. "This time I literally had to go through a secret passageway."

"I don't even need to ask who that is," Reese said.

Richard tapped his Gucci watch. "Chop, chop, ladies. We're out of here."

I stood up. "We just got here. We haven't even toured the property."

"No need." Richard waved a handful of catering folders. "I got all the information and ran though all the reception rooms. It's perfect. Hailey will love it."

Kate ended her call and dropped her phone into her bag. "That's it? We haven't even been to our rooms or tasted the food."

"Let's see." Richard put his hands on his hips. "We can stay overnight and risk being murdered in our sleep when those old birds catch up with us, or we can leave for Dublin now and increase our chances of surviving the night. I, for one, would prefer not to be strangled or bashed over the head."

"That's good enough for me," Kate said, heading for the door. "Dublin, here I come."

"I'd better go," I said to Reese. "It looks like we're going to be doing the express version of the rest of our trip."

"You're heading to Dublin now?" Reese asked.

"I'm guessing Richard worked his magic and got the hotel to let us check in a day early," I said, watching Richard spin on his heel and disappear into the library. "I can tell he's in no mood to accept a four-star hotel."

"Be careful, babe. I want you back in one piece."

I headed for the door and twisted my head to take one final look at the beautiful water cascade, my eyes hesitating as I saw two people walking under the portico at the top of the hill. "That's odd."

"To want you back safely?"

"No." I shook my head and squinted into the distance, but the figures must have moved behind the columns. "I thought I saw something."

"Annabelle." Reese sounded worried. "You aren't making sense."

"It's nothing. My mind is playing tricks on me." I turned away and walked out of the conservatory and into the massive library with black columns and gold chandeliers. The flash of curly blond hair could have been anyone, I told myself.

27

"But you can't be sure?" Richard asked me for the tenth time since we'd left Ballyfin Demesne, leaning into the aisle of the van since we were sitting across from each other.

"Of course I can't," I said, keeping one eye on him and one on Buster, who was white-knuckling the steering wheel since we'd entered Dublin. "Like I told you before, the blond curly hair I saw was all the way across the lawn. But for a moment, I thought it might be Grace and they might have followed us."

"Why?" Fern's head popped up from the seat cushion behind me. "Why would the newlyweds have any reason to follow us if one of the old ladies is smuggling Irish artifacts?"

"We're sure Grace and Derek weren't outside when we left Dromoland?" Kate asked, her head appearing beside Fern's.

"I didn't see them," I said.

"Me neither." Fern shook his head. "And I made sure to hug everyone before leaving."

I clutched the leather armrest as Buster took a roundabout while Mack called out directions. "After this, take your next left."

The sun had set, but the city of Dublin was by no means

dark. Compared to the quiet countryside we'd been driving through all week, the city was bustling with energy and noise. I looked out the window as we crossed over the river. The reflections of street lamps glowed in long streaks across the rippled surface of the water. Even without the windows open, I could hear the hum of the pubs as we turned onto a busy street.

"Even if it was them, we didn't see anyone tearing out of the estate after us," Kate said, dropping her voice. "I'm pretty sure from the way Buster's been driving, we would have lost anyone who tried it anyway."

We all lurched to one side as we took a sharp turn.

"Doesn't everyone and their brother have our trip itinerary, thanks to Fern?" I asked as Fern's head disappeared from view.

"But aren't we arriving here a day early?" Kate asked.

"Yes," I admitted, "but I feel like that's not a foolproof way to shake people off our trail."

Richard waved his hands. "None of that matters. First thing tomorrow, Annabelle is calling the Gardaí and we're handing over our evidence."

I started to agree, then paused. "Wait, why do I have to be the one to call? I didn't take the bag or open it."

"You're the one with all the experience dealing with law enforcement," Richard said. "You know I'm still experiencing PTPD."

I narrowed my gaze at him. "And that would be what exactly?"

He loosened the collar of his shirt. "Post Traumatic Police Disorder. My skin has been a mess since the Gardaí showed up at Dromoland."

"I'm pretty sure bad skin isn't a symptom of post traumatic stress," I said.

His eyes widened. "Annabelle, I am on the verge of a rash here."

"I'm happy to talk with the police if they're all as cute as Garda Ryan," Kate said.

"I'll call," I said, knowing that if Kate was in charge and the garda was cute, she might forget about returning the artifacts entirely. "I'll do anything if I can get a good night's sleep first."

"Your wish is my command," Buster said, bringing the van to an abrupt stop.

We all looked up at the stately five-story brick hotel. Spotlights illuminated the first few floors and the ornate stucco detailing above the arched windows. A wide glass canopy extended over the entrance, and above that were stone window boxes overflowing with greenery and the flag of Ireland fluttering in the breeze.

"Hallelujah," Richard said, putting his man bag across his shoulder. "I can smell the five-star service from here."

Buster opened the van doors and we all filed out as several bellmen rushed forward to unload the luggage, and a doorman in tails and a top hat directed us to the revolving wooden entrance. I breathed deeply as we walked into the marble foyer with white columns and a crystal chandelier. A dark wood credenza to one side held a massive display of green-and-white flowers in front of a gilded mirror, which explained why the air smelled of lilies.

I hitched my black bag higher as I walked past the columns toward the black-and-gold staircase adorned with a candelabra. I glanced up to the second floor, which seemed to be a collection of green-and-white arches and more glittering chandeliers.

"I've died and gone to heaven," Richard said, taking in the obvious luxury. "You all stay here while I go get our keys."

I didn't argue while he disappeared, but I did look for a place to sit.

"Come on." Kate motioned for me to follow her up the stairs. "Let's explore a little."

"Can't I just explore with my eyes?" I asked. Even though we'd been on the van for the past two hours, I felt worn out from the chaos and stress of the trip.

Kate got halfway up the staircase and put a hand on her hip.

"I thought we were supposed to be checking this out as a potential wedding venue?"

"Low blow," I muttered, but followed her anyway with Fern, Buster, and Mack right behind me. After assisting me for years, she definitely knew my weak spots.

We reached the landing and my eyes were drawn to a set of open doors leading into a room that looked like a cross between a bar and a library. On the other side of the landing was a short staircase leading to an open-air terrace.

"We're going to check out the terrace," Mack said as he and Buster continued to the short flight of stairs. "I love decorating outdoor spaces."

"We'll be in the bar," Fern said, making a beeline for the dark, clubby room.

A large oil painting of a man hung in a gold frame over a fireplace on the far wall, and the rest of the walls alternated bookshelves and dark wood paneling. A hunter-green leather bar occupied one half of the room with green leather furniture groupings taking up the rest. Shelving behind the bar held bottles of champagne, each single bottle occupying its own shelf.

"This is a change from all the white and green," Kate said, plopping down on a high-backed green sofa. "I like it."

"Is there anything more Irish than books and booze together?" I asked, approaching one of the shelves and running a finger across the spines of the books.

"This would be a great spot for groomsmen photos," Kate said, swiveling her head. "Can't you just imagine having the guys each perched on one of the barstools?"

"Remember we're trying to cut down on the groomsmen drinking before the weddings?" I said.

"Where's the fun in that?" Fern asked, eying the champagne bottles on the wall.

"You didn't have to seat half the guests at the last wedding because the groomsmen forgot to come back to the church in time," I told him as I sat down on a red leather barstool. "Kate and I ended up being the stand-in ushers because the ushers and groomsmen were tying one on at the bar around the corner."

Kate wrinkled her nose. "I did not like being an usher. Guests can be so demanding."

"Good luck planning a wedding in Ireland where the bridal party doesn't drink," Fern said, sinking down into the couch next to Kate.

"I don't mind if they drink," I said. "I just want them to do it after the ceremony."

"Agreed," Kate said. "I hate sending drunk groomsmen down the aisle."

"Or priests," I said, remembering a wedding not so long ago where the priest had been the one to over imbibe and pass out mid ceremony.

"You always have me as a stand-in," Fern reminded me. "I don't know when I've had as much fun as I did when I got to be the priest for that wedding."

The thought of Fern's ad-libbed ceremony still made me cringe. It may have been the only wedding ceremony in the history of the world that mentioned bad hair days and the importance of moisturizing. "Let's hope that was a one-off."

"Do you think this is a working bar?" Fern asked, licking his lips.

"Considering there's no bartender, I'd say no," Kate said.

"No worries." Fern produced his flask from the pocket of his brown flannel pants. "I'm prepared for any emergency."

He popped up and bustled over behind the bar, bending over then placing a pair of cut glass rocks glasses on top of the curved bar. After locating a few more glasses, he began pouring out Irish whiskey from his flask.

I glanced out the open doors, but didn't see anyone coming. I suppose it wasn't a crime to borrow the hotel's glasses if we were using our own whiskey.

"Whose idea was it to leave the lobby?" Richard asked,

flouncing into the room and leaning on the padded edge of the bar to catch his breath. "I had no idea where you'd gone."

"Sorry," I said, patting the barstool next to mine. "We were checking out the event spaces."

"Let me pour you a drink," Fern said, producing another glass from under the bar.

Richard blinked a few times. "Was I gone so long Fern actually got a job at the hotel?"

Fern slid the glass over to Richard and fluttered a hand in the air. "Aren't you a stitch? This bar isn't staffed, so we helped ourselves to the glassware."

Kate joined us at the bar while Fern passed out the remaining glasses and lifted his glass into the air. "A toast."

"To our first destination wedding," Kate said.

I lifted my glass. "Slainte."

Richard clinked his glass with mine. "And to no little old ladies killing us in our sleep."

I took a sip, feeling the Irish whiskey burning my throat as I swallowed. My phone buzzed in my bag, and I pulled it out. "What does Leatrice want? I hope she's reconsidered the orange lace bridesmaids' jumpsuits."

Kate nearly choked on her whiskey. "Orange lace? Jumpsuits? Which poor friends of hers have to wear that?"

I realized I'd forgotten to mention both the horrific outfits and the fact that Leatrice had chosen us as attendants. "Actually, we do."

Kate gaped at me. "By 'we' I hope you mean you and Richard."

"Not on your life," Richard said. "My jumpsuit days are over."

The fact that Richard had ever had jumpsuit days made me want to stop and ask him to elaborate, but the phone continued to buzz. “Didn’t I mention that we’re both bridesmaids?”

Kate slipped off the stool, barely catching herself before she landed on the floor.

I clicked the talk button. "Hey, Leatrice. How's it going?"

"Everything's fine, dearie. I wanted to double-check that the plant on your desk is fake."

I'd found an adorable pot of fake lavender at Target, and thought it perfectly fit my level of horticultural prowess. "It is, but why are you asking?"

"I didn't want to water it if it doesn't need water," she said as if my question was the silliest thing she'd ever heard.

"Okay," I said, putting a finger to one ear to block the sound of Kate's spluttering protests in the background, "but why would you be in my apartment watering my fake plant?"

"Oh goodness," Leatrice said. "What time is it over there?"

"Why does that matter?" I asked. "Leatrice, have you been using Sharpies again? You know the fumes make you loopy."

"No, nothing like that, I promise. It's just . . . Oh, dear."

Kate mumbled something about hating lace as she walked with her rocks glass to the open double doors leading into the bar. "I'm going to check out the terrace with Buster and Mack while you . . . Is that . . .?"

I turned to watch her gaze drop to the entrance of the hotel and my stomach clenched. Had the old ladies tracked us down already or were the newlyweds on our tail as I suspected?

Kate turned to me, her eyes wide. "I can't believe it."

When I joined her at the door, I almost dropped my drink. That made two of us.

28

I rolled over in bed, shielding my eyes from the light streaming in through the sheer curtains. It was clearly morning, but how late had I slept? I reached across the king-sized bed and felt around for my phone on the nightstand, flipping it up and groaning when I saw that it was past nine o'clock. So much for getting an early start on the day. Not that anyone would expect me to be bounding out of bed after our surprise the night before.

"Good morning, sleepyhead."

I sat up as Mike Reese walked into the room holding two paper to-go coffee cups. He wore black athletic shorts and a white Under Armor T-shirt, and his face was flushed with one dark loop of hair falling down over his forehead.

"So I didn't imagine you," I said, flopping back onto the down pillows. "You weren't a mirage created by my travel-addled brain?"

He crossed the room, dropping a newspaper on the dove-gray armchair by the window before sitting beside me on the edge of the bed. "If I'm a mirage, then I'm a very interactive one."

I felt my cheeks warm as he leaned down to kiss me. "I can't believe you let me sleep so late. Did you actually go running?"

"The hotel is right across from St. Stephen's Green. It's a great place for a morning run." He handed me one of the coffee cups and cocked an eyebrow. "I didn't let you sleep late; you were comatose when I tried to wake you earlier."

"If you tried to entice me by mentioning a run, then that's why." I took a sip of the coffee, enjoying the flavor of mocha and the instant warmth. "How can you be so energetic after flying six hours yesterday?"

"More than that," he said, taking a sip of his own coffee, which I knew was not augmented by mocha and sugar and whipped cream like mine. "I had to fly to New York first to catch the daytime flight."

I wrapped an arm around his waist and leaned into him. "Thanks for coming. I feel so much better now that you're here."

"Like I said, Ireland is the type of place I wanted to visit with you. The fact that you're knee-deep in a potentially life-threatening criminal investigation only sped up my timetable." He brushed a strand of hair off my face. "I was serious when I said I wanted you back in one piece."

I felt a slight flutter in my belly as I put my coffee down on the polished wood nightstand. "And am I correct in remembering that Richard was in cahoots with you about this?"

"Cahoots makes us sound like co-conspirators."

"Which you are," I said. "I'm assuming you two cooked this up when you were on the phone the other night."

He laughed. "If by 'cooked this up' you mean he told me the name of your Dublin hotel and when you'd be arriving, then yes, he helped me cook up my surprise visit."

"Remind me to thank him later." I pulled him down for another kiss. "A lot later."

The knock at the door made me reluctantly pull away.

"I guess we couldn't expect your merry gang to stay away for too long," Reese said with a sigh.

I tossed back the white duvet and slipped out of bed, padding to the bathroom and snagging the terry cloth hotel robe off the back of the door. "I'm amazed they held out this long."

Reese walked to the door and glanced out the peephole before opening it. "I guess it could be worse. It's only one."

Richard strode in with the fake Louis Vuitton bag thrown over his shoulder. "Is she decent?"

"Of course I'm decent," I said, walking toward him.

Richard gave me a quick once-over. "Barely, darling." He looked pointedly at his watch. "Did you just roll out of bed?"

I ran a hand through my hair. "Not just." I motioned to my boyfriend. "And he's been up for hours."

Richard took in Reese's slightly sweaty attire and arched an eyebrow. "I can see that. Someone's hitting the ground running."

"So is this my personal wake-up call, or did you have something specific to talk about?" I asked. Now that I was up and slightly caffeinated, I was dying for a shower.

He swung the designer duffel down and set it on the round wooden table positioned next to the gray armchair. "In all the excitement of your surprise visitor, did you forget about this?"

"Of course not." I hadn't forgotten about it exactly, but I'd been happily distracted since Reese had shown up. It was almost the first time since we'd arrived I hadn't been worrying about someone getting killed or attacked or framed for murder, so I didn't feel too guilty about it.

Reese walked over to the bag. "I take it these are the artifacts?"

Richard nodded. "I insisted on keeping them in my room last night." He gave me a knowing look. "I couldn't be sure Fern wouldn't start accessorizing with them."

Reese unzipped the bag and unrolled a few of the tea towels. "They look pretty old. I did some searching before I left and did find some reports of thefts taking place around Ireland in some of the smaller museums and stately homes."

"Any in County Limerick or Galway?" I asked.

Reese grinned at me. "Funny you should mention it, but yes."

Richard clapped his hands together. "There you have it. Case closed."

"Except we have no idea who actually took them and what they were planning on doing with them," I reminded him. "It doesn't do us much good to rescue these if the thief is able to do it again."

"I wouldn't say you have no idea," Reese said, zipping up the bag again. "You've successfully narrowed the potential suspects."

Richard tapped a toe on the carpet. "To every old lady in the genealogy tour group."

"And possibly the newlyweds, although they're admittedly a long shot," I added.

Reese glanced from me to Richard and back to me. "Might I remind you it isn't your job to track down the guilty party or even to figure out why they did it? All we need to do is return the stolen artifacts and let the local garda handle the rest."

Richard and I both let out a breath, but his sounded like it was from relief and mine was from exasperation. We were supposed to walk away from the case without finding out who was behind the murder of Colleen, the attack on Nancy, and Kate being framed for murder?

"I know what you're thinking, Annabelle." Richard flicked his eyes to me. "The thought of leaving without solving the case makes your skin crawl. You're a born problem solver. It's what makes you such a good wedding planner, but it's also what gets you into so much trouble."

"I never get into trouble," I said.

Reese made a strangled sound and tried to cover it up with a cough.

Richard held up his fingers. "Should I list off the times you've almost gotten killed?"

I pulled myself up to my full height. "That won't be necessary, thank you very much. I get your point."

"Do I need to remind you that we're here to find the perfect wedding venue for the biggest wedding of the year?" Richard said. "We only have a few more days before we go home, so I suggest we get this bag to the authorities and get back to work. Our *real* work."

I knew Richard was right, as much as I hated to admit it. My instinct to fix things--from upset brides to missing bouquets to unsolved murders--was usually a good thing, but not when the compulsion overtook everything else. I knew it drove Reese crazy too, and I'd honestly tried to rein it in. Not always with great success.

I threw up my hands. "You're right. Hailey is expecting a full report on all the venues we've seen as soon as we get home. I need to take photos of this hotel and pop into the reception spaces, even though I have a feeling she's going to choose one of the sites in the country."

Reese stepped closer and wrapped an arm around my waist. "You know what they say about all work and no play. Don't you think we should see a little of Dublin while we're here?"

I felt my shoulders relax as I leaned into him. "You're right. Especially since you flew all this way."

"There's a Gardaí station at Trinity College," Reese said. "I already checked it out on a map. We can walk through Grafton Street on our way to return the artifacts. Maybe have a leisurely lunch on the way back?"

"Now you're talking," Richard said. "Shall we meet downstairs in half an hour?"

Reese dropped his eyes to me and grinned. I knew he'd probably hoped to have lunch by ourselves, but I wasn't going to be the one to tell Richard to take a hike.

"We both still need to shower and dress," I said.

Richard raised an eyebrow. "I've seen you get ready, darling. Cats have more time-intensive grooming regimens."

Reese tugged me closer. "I hope the shower is big enough for two if Richard's rushing us like this."

Richard's face flushed as he spun on his heel. "An hour then, but not a moment longer. The sooner we get rid of this bag, the better."

I looked up at my boyfriend after Richard had flounced out of the room, the door clicking shut behind him. "So the quickest way to get rid of Richard is to suggest we shower together. That's good to know for future reference. You think it would work the same way on Leatrice?"

"Doubtful," Reese said. "She'd probably stand outside the door trying to hand us rubber ducks."

I laughed. I knew this probably wasn't far from the truth.

"So," I motioned to the bathroom with my head. "You want first shower?"

His eyes met mine and he grinned wickedly. "Oh, I wasn't kidding about the shower being big enough for two. We do have an hour, after all."

This trip was finally looking up.

29

"Well, that was anticlimactic," I said as we walked out of the Trinity College Gardaí station.

Richard twisted his neck to look back at the gray stone building with its three wide archways over the door. "What did you expect?"

"They seemed grateful to have the artifacts returned and took down your statements," Reese said as he took my hand in his.

"I don't know," I said, dodging a group of people on the sidewalk. "I got the feeling they weren't convinced by Richard's explanation of how we ended up with a fake Louis Vuitton bag."

"The ten minutes on the differences in stitching might have been a bit much," Reese said, not looking at Richard.

"I thought they would appreciate the detail," Richard said. "Don't police like to be thorough?"

We walked around the stone walls of Trinity College as we headed back to Grafton Street. Richard had insisted we walk briskly to the station and rid ourselves of the fake Louis before stopping to enjoy any of the street performers or cafes. I pushed up the sleeves of my black cardigan. It wasn't warm by DC standards, but the sun was peeking out from behind gray clouds, and it must have been nearing mid-day.

"Do you think they're going to try to figure out who's doing the stealing and smuggling?" I asked. Although the gardas had been polite, I got the feeling they weren't all that concerned by a thieving band of Americans, if that's who was behind everything. Even when I'd explained about the murder and attack, they'd only raised a few eyebrows and jotted down the name of Garda Ryan to contact for further information.

"How exactly could they do that?" Richard asked. "Start chasing the old ladies around the country? Even we have no idea which of the women could have murdered Colleen and attacked Nancy. Not to mention lift a bunch of antiquities—if it's all connected."

I stopped in the middle of the sidewalk and stared at him. "Of course it's all connected. What are the chances all of these things would happen during a single trip and not be related?"

Richard shrugged. "With our luck? Relatively high."

We turned onto the pedestrian-filled Grafton Street that wound its way down to St. Stephen's Green. I could hear singers busking for money and smell the scent of lunch wafting from the pubs and cafes. Both sides of the street were lined with four-and-five-story brownstone-style buildings, some redbrick and others gray stone with storefronts at the bottom. Smaller shops with narrow awnings were interspersed with larger chain stores advertising sales in their glass windows.

"Is that Mack?" Reese asked, and I followed his line of sight down the street.

Buster and Mack didn't blend in with most surroundings, so I wasn't surprised to see that it was indeed our leather-clad friend coming out of a shop, bags hanging from his arms. Buster was right behind him and was equally laden with paper shopping bags. A few people stepped out of their way and more than a few mouths dropped open as the men lumbered down the street.

"Buster!" I yelled. "Mack!"

They turned and grinned when they saw us.

"You caught us," Mack said when we'd joined them. He held up a plastic cup. "We were getting ice cream."

I glanced at the blue-and-white storefront they'd emerged from. Murphy's Ice Cream was a small shop with a drawing of an ice cream cone beside its name, and it proclaimed that it was "handmade in Dingle."

"How is it?" Reese asked, eyeing the gooey concoction in Mack's dish.

"Amazing," Mack said. "I got the Dreamy Creamy Caramel."

My stomach rumbled. "We probably should eat real food before ice cream."

"Why?" Reese asked, winking at me and disappearing into the shop.

Richard followed him mumbling something about culinary research.

"So what did you find?" I asked Buster and Mack, pointing to their bags.

"Clothes for baby Merry," Buster said, placing one armful of bags on the ground and handing his ice cream to Mack.

"She's going to be the most stylish baby in the city," Mack said, taking a bite from his ice cream and then from Buster's.

Buster held up a small fisherman's sweater with tiny nut-brown buttons. "Isn't it perfect?"

"We got it a bit big," Mack explained, "since she won't wear it until next fall."

Buster replaced the sweater in the bag and took his ice cream back, narrowing his eyes at Mack when he noticed the missing bite. "What have you been up to?"

Mack nudged me. "Aside from a happy reunion with the detective."

I felt my cheeks warm. They were undoubtedly referring to how I'd jumped on Reese when I'd seen him the night before, wrapping my legs around his waist and nearly knocking him over.

Kate and Fern had cheered, while Richard had sucked in air so sharply I'd thought he might keel over himself.

"We were at the Gardaí station," I said, "returning the stolen artifacts and giving them statements."

"That's a relief," Mack said through a mouthful of ice cream. "So we don't need to worry about it anymore."

"I suppose not," I said, although I still hadn't convinced myself I could forget about everything that had happened.

"One Sticky Toffee Pudding and one Dingle Sea Salt," Reese said, reappearing from inside the shop and holding out two plastic cups. "Take your pick, babe."

"I'll take the sea salt." I took the ice cream not covered in toffee sauce and took a bite. It was creamy and sweet with a salty tang.

"What did you get?" Buster asked Richard when he came out.

"Dingle Gin," Richard said. "Something you can't get in DC."

Mack goggled at the dish. "I've never heard of gin ice cream."

Richard took a bite and smiled. "Delicious."

We resumed walking down the street eating our ice cream. My eyes caught a souvenir shop, its windows a riot of green with Irish flags, stuffed sheep, and leprechauns.

"Should we get something for Leatrice?" I asked.

Richard shuddered. "The last thing we need is Leatrice running around in a 'Kiss Me I'm Irish' apron or a shamrock hat."

"If you want something more subtle, we can show you where we got Merry's sweater," Mack said. "The Aran Sweater Market is just ahead."

"I'd rather her be dressed like an Irish fisherman than a leprechaun," Richard said.

We passed a woman in a short black skirt dancing to festive Irish music from a boom box, her feet flying while the rest of her stayed perfectly straight. I turned to watch her as we passed and nearly walked into a tall black streetlamp in the middle of the street.

Reese caught me by the elbow and steered me around it with one hand. "Eyes on the road, babe."

Before I could thank him, I was almost knocked off my feet. It took me a moment to realize it was Kate who'd run smack into me. She held me by both arms, and I felt glad I'd finished my ice cream since the dish lay on the ground.

"Thank goodness," she said as she gasped for breath.

Fern was right behind her, his hands on his knees as he sucked in air. "We ran . . . all the way . . . from the hotel."

"What on earth is wrong with you two?" Richard asked, putting a palm to his heart. "You almost scared me to death." His eyes lingered on Fern. "Do I dare ask what you're wearing?"

Fern perked up as his eyes dropped to his saffron-yellow kilt with green shamrocks down one side and hunter-green blazer atop it. "An Irish Saffron kilt."

"I thought kilts were green plaid," Reese said to me.

"A common misconception," Fern said between breaths. "This type of kilt was first worn by the Irish military, and it's the most popular kilt design in Ireland now." He touched a hand to the shamrocks along the front pleat and winked at us. "I had it custom made to my measurements. I'm a perfect size eight, by the way."

Kate stamped one high-heeled boot on the gray paving stones. "Fern! Focus!" Her eyes scanned all of us. "Where's the Louis Vuitton bag?"

"The fake one," Fern added.

"We just handed it over to the Gardai," Reese said in the cop voice he used to get people to talk. "Do you want to explain what's going on?"

Kate sagged against me. "Good. At least they can't get it."

"Who can't get it?" I asked, looking over Kate's shoulder to see if someone was chasing her. I saw nothing but fellow shoppers and tourists meandering down the street.

"The other Americans," she said. "The old ladies."

"What about them?" Richard asked. "Don't you think you two are being a bit hysterical?"

Kate swung her head around to him. "People in gas houses shouldn't throw stones."

"Do you mean *glass* houses?" Richard asked with a tortured sigh.

She gave her head a quick shake. "Who builds glass houses?"

I waved Richard off before he could argue with her. Kate's ability to mangle phrases was legendary, and I suspected she now did it just to get under his skin.

"You were saying something about the American women on the genealogy tour?" Reese said, trying to steer the conversation back to the subject at hand.

Fern nodded. "They just showed up at the hotel."

My stomach tightened. "Our hotel? The Shelbourne?"

"We just watched them all check in," Kate said, her face grim.

30

"I can't believe it," Richard said, sinking further down against the dark wood paneling. "We're fugitives from our own hotel."

I looked over my shoulder, even though we'd closed the door to the pub's snug after we'd all piled into the small, private room at the front of Kehoe's. Shifting on the short leather stool and readjusting my legs under the battered wooden table, I was glad we'd ducked down a side street and into the traditional Irish pub before anyone else went into full panic mode. We'd been even luckier that the pub's snug, the small room right off the front door that had once been used by women and clergy and anyone not wanting to be spotted drinking, had been available.

"We're hardly fugitives," I said, dropping my voice and smiling up at the ruddy-cheeked bartender who'd entered the room and began doling out pints of Guinness, shots of whiskey, and glasses of water. It was a bit early for me to have a pint, but after the recent revelation, I wasn't going to stand in the way of anyone who might need something to calm their nerves. At least it was technically afternoon. Only a few minutes after, but after nonetheless.

The pub wasn't busy yet, but there were a few patrons talking at the long wooden bar right outside the snug, and I could hear the muffled sounds of a singer crooning "When Irish Eyes Are Smiling" on the sidewalk. Like most pubs I'd been in so far, the air in Kehoe's held the lingering scent of the dark beer it served. Even though I wasn't a big beer drinker, the smell was oddly comforting.

Reese waited until the door was closed again and he'd taken a sip of his Guinness before turning to Fern and Kate. "Let's take it again from the beginning."

Fern swirled the contents of his rocks glass of Jameson and nodded. "Kate and I were coming downstairs to head out for a little shopping."

"And grab some lunch," Kate added, leaning back against the wall and crossing her legs, exposing bare skin between where her boots left off and her pink minidress began.

"Speaking of food," Mack said, craning his neck around the room, "you don't suppose this place serves any, do you?"

"You just had ice cream," Richard said.

Buster readjusted himself on the long brown leather bench that abutted the wall and ran down the length of the snug. "That was a late breakfast."

I took a sip of water and focused on Fern "So, as you were saying, you'd just come downstairs."

"We were walking through the lobby where you check in," he said, tossing back his drink and placing the empty glass on the table. "That's when we saw her."

"Her who?" Richard asked.

"Myrna," Kate said, taking a drink of her Guinness and dabbing at the foam left on her upper lip.

"She's the tour group leader," I reminded my boyfriend since he hadn't had direct dealings with any of the ladies.

"Anyone else?" Richard asked. "Maybe the entire group isn't with her."

"Oh, they're all here," Kate said. "I snuck into the front foyer and saw a few of them in the lounge right off the entrance. Plus, their bus was outside unloading bags."

"Just you?" Reese asked.

Fern pulled his flask out of the pocket of his green jacket and waved a hand at his yellow kilt and knee-high socks with matching yellow tassels. "I can't exactly blend in this, detective."

I scanned our group: two burly bald men in head-to-toe black leather, a blonde in a Lily Pulitzer mini-dress, and a man with a man bun wearing a yellow kilt . Even the most hardened city dweller would do a double take.

"I'm glad you're aware of that," Richard said. "How did you get out of the hotel unseen? I doubt there was a fife-and-drum convention you could pretend to be a part of."

"A back exit," Kate said, giving me a knowing look. "Every hotel has a back entrance or loading dock."

One advantage to being an event planner was that you got used to navigating the back of house in any hotel. Kate was right. There was always an employee entrance or loading dock where trucks made deliveries.

"So you're sure they didn't see you?" Reese asked.

"Pretty sure," Kate said, "but they must know we're here. Why else would they show up the day after we do? And right after we discover that we've taken one of their bags?"

"It might be because of the genealogy concierge," Richard said.

Every head swiveled toward him.

"The what?" Buster asked.

Richard sighed. "Does no one else read guidebooks? The Shelbourne Hotel is known for having a dedicated concierge who assists tourists in finding their Irish roots. It only makes sense that a tour focused on genealogy would be interested in that. Plus, we already know the old ladies are well-heeled, so I doubt the expense would bother them."

Now that he mentioned it, I recalled reading something on

the hotel's website about the genealogy concierge, but I'd been more focused on the size of the event space.

Fern poured a healthy amount of amber liquid from his flask into his emptied glass. "So you're saying it could be a complete coincidence that they're here?"

Richard shrugged. "What are the chances they would be able to show up and get that many rooms at the last minute?"

"So what do we do?" I asked, more to Reese than to anyone else. "If the thief and murderer thinks we have the bag and knows we're in the hotel, we're all in danger."

"Then we make sure they know we don't have the bag," Richard said.

"What if they don't believe us?" Kate said, her voice quivering. "Criminals aren't the most trusting types. If they were desperate enough to kill one person and attack another, don't you think they'd make sure we weren't bluffing?"

Fern choked on his drink. "You mean they'd still come after us even though we don't have the bag or artifacts?"

I looked to Reese to argue, but his brow was furrowed.

"As much as I hate to admit it, Kate makes some good points," he said. "We aren't dealing with a rational person. They probably know *they'd* never turn in a bag filled with valuables, so they'd doubt that anyone else would either. Dishonest people are the least trusting because they expect the world to think and behave as badly as they do."

"That's discouraging," Mack said.

Reese shrugged. "I'm afraid I have a cynical world view after years of dealing with criminals."

"So we need to sneak out of the hotel, rebook earlier flights, and never return to Ireland," Richard said, pulling out his phone. "I'll see what flights are available this afternoon."

"That doesn't mean they can't track us down," I said. "If those items were worth killing over, they very well might be worth a trip to DC."

Fern gave a small squeak and put his hands to his cheeks.

"Do you think we'll need to change our names and get cosmetic surgery?"

"Let's not jump to conclusions," Reese said. "We still don't know for sure that one of the ladies is behind the stolen antiquities or the attacks."

I rapped my fingers on the wooden table. "You're right. We need to figure out who's behind all this."

Kate nodded. "I won't sleep soundly until we know for sure who could be coming for us."

Buster folded his arms across his chest. "So we draw out the killer."

"We've done that before," Mack said.

Reese held up his hands. "Wait a second. That's not what I meant at all." His eyes slid to me. "Is this how you all end up in so many crazy situations?"

"It's not crazy," I said. "Can you tell me you're 100 percent certain the thief and killer won't come after us?"

He hesitated.

"See?" I said. "We're in danger until we know who's behind everything, and I didn't get the idea the Gardaí were going to put much muscle behind this."

"The question is, how will we draw out the thief?" Kate asked. "We don't have the artifacts anymore."

"But they don't know that," Richard said.

Fern bounced up and down in his seat. "That's right. They can't even tell the difference between a real and fake Louis. And we still have the real one."

"No." Reese shook his head firmly. "I do not like where this is going."

I leaned forward. "We spread the word that we're meeting the police to hand over the bag tonight in the hotel."

"Then we lay a trap when the killer shows up before the police," Kate said.

"Set a trap?" Reese spluttered. "You want to encourage a killer to come after you?"

"That's where you come in." I squeezed his arm. "You'll be somewhere nearby in case things go south."

"Things have already gone south," he muttered.

"It's perfect." I leaned into him. "None of the women know what you look like, so they'll have no clue you're with us."

Fern gave him a slow wink. "You're one of us now, sweetie."

Reese drained half of his Guinness.

"I'm with the detective. This is begging for trouble." Richard held a finger over his phone. "I say we book the new tickets and change our identities. I hear Mexico is a nice place to lay low."

Fern nibbled the edge of his thumbnail. "I guess I could get used to going by my drag name, Tequila Sunrise."

"Come on," Kate said. "Don't you want to see Colleen's killer caught?"

Reese sighed. “You aren’t going to let this go, are you?”

“Not if we’re still in danger,” I said. “I don’t want to be looking over my shoulder for a sinister old lady for the rest of my life.”

Richard shuddered. “That’s a terrifying thought considering we already have a crazy old lady back home.”

Reese clunked his pint glass back onto the table. "Then if we're going to do this, we're going to do it right so no one is at risk." He put his forearms against the table and bent forward. "Here's the plan."

Fern looked around the table before leaning in. "An official plan by a real cop. This is so exciting."

Richard arched an eyebrow at me. "I think we may have broken your boyfriend, darling."

31

"Are we sure the man who came up with this plan is really Mike Reese?" Kate asked as we sat in the upstairs library bar at The Shelbourne Hotel. "Is it possible he's been taken by aliens and his body replaced?"

"I'm as surprised as you are," I told her as I readjusted the Louis Vuitton duffel bag by my feet.

We'd selected the 1824 Bar as our fake meeting spot with the Gardaí because it wasn't a working bar, and it had easy access to stairs as well as the nearby terrace where Reese and Richard were positioned out of sight. Fern was on the staircase landing above us, and Buster and Mack were outside the hotel. From the intimate, wood-paneled room, Kate and I had a view of the entrance of the hotel as well as the main staircase.

"I guess we're rubbing off on him," Kate said, swiveling around on the barstool so she faced the door.

"Wearing him down is more like it," I said. Reese had made me promise that once we'd found out who was behind the smuggling and attacks, we'd take the last two days of the trip to do nothing but sleep late and explore Dublin. "I think he knows that I won't be happy until the case is solved."

"All I have to say is don't let go of him, Annabelle. You've found a guy who thinks your obsessive problem-solving is endearing and doesn't mind that you can't cook. There may not be another one like him in the entire DC metropolitan area."

"Thanks, I think." I grinned in spite of her double-edged compliment. I knew she was right. Reese was the perfect guy for me, and if I was being completely immodest, I thought I was pretty good for him too. Even though we had only been living together for a few months, it felt odd to think back to what life had been like before he was an everyday part of it.

"I know we want to get more destination weddings," Kate said, "but I'm ready to get back home. Traveling is exhausting even without being accused of murder."

"I hear you. The idea of planning destination weddings is better than the reality."

"No kidding." Kate spun to face me. "They never show jet-lagged people or damaged luggage in photo spreads for weddings overseas."

I watched a few people walk up from the entrance foyer, but I didn't recognize them. I knew we were still about ten minutes early for our supposed meeting, but I expected the real smuggler to show her face before the Gardaí arrived. I tapped my foot on the maroon carpeting.

"When you and Reese get married, do you want it to be in DC or someplace exotic?" Kate asked.

I nearly slipped off my stool and instinctively glanced around, afraid that my boyfriend had somehow heard her from the terrace. "Who says we're getting married?"

She angled her head at me. "You've been dating for a while;you've been living together for a few months; you're clearly crazy for each other. Why wouldn't you get married?"

An excellent question, I thought. Why wouldn't we? And why did the thought of me being the one to walk down the aisle seem to fluster me so badly? Was I so used to being on the other side of things that I couldn't imagine being the girl in the white dress?

"Don't tell me planning weddings has ruined them for you," Kate said, eyeing me. "Just because our brides are crazy, doesn't mean you'll lose your sanity when it's your turn."

That was a scary thought. It had never occurred to me I could become a bridezilla. "It's not that."

"Are you a wedding planner who doesn't believe in marriage?" Kate lowered her voice. "That would be so weird."

"You're telling me you still believe in the fairy tale after all the craziness we've seen?"

Kate nodded, her blond hair bouncing. "Absolutely. I plan to get married."

"You do?" I couldn't keep the surprise out of my voice.

"I want someone sexy, smart, and rich." She counted off three fingers. "It may take three different husbands to get all that, but I'm willing to go the extra mile."

I laughed. "If business is slow, I guess we can always fall back on planning your weddings."

"You know me." She gave me an arch smile. "Always willing to take one for the team."

I glanced up at the next staircase landing where we'd stationed Fern. He'd declined to take off his kilt, saying it helped him blend in, despite the fact that he was the only person in the hotel--Irish or not--wearing a yellow kilt. At least it made him easier to spot. He gave me a thumbs-up.

Fern had been in charge of getting the word out to the American ladies about our find and our meeting, his ability to disseminate gossip far and wide finally coming in handy. He'd spotted them having tea in The Lord Mayor's Lounge earlier and promptly joined them. After regaling them with his story of the artifacts and our upcoming meeting to turn them over to the authorities, he'd left them with mouths hanging open.

I turned to the walls of dark-wood shelving and the bottles of champagne tucked in each one. I could go for a drink right about now, I thought.

"You've got to be kidding me," Kate said, causing me to pull my attention from the shelving behind the bar and follow her line of sight.

She was looking wide-eyed at a what appeared to be a bridal party descending the staircase with the bride in front and several bridesmaids in lavender dresses holding her train. A cluster of children in white outfits brought up the rear.

"It doesn't matter where we go," Kate muttered. "We are stalked by weddings."

I fought the urge to straighten the bride's twisted veil as she and her party walked onto the terrace. "You don't think they're having the wedding there, do you?"

Kate put a hand to her mouth. "If they are, it's going to be a challenge for Reese and Richard to stay there."

I wondered what my boyfriend and best friend were doing now that a wedding had overrun their hiding place.

Kate nudged me, pointing up at Fern. "And the hits keep coming."

"Impossible," I whispered as I realized he was talking to the newlyweds from the plane who'd been showing up throughout our trip.

"We may have been wrong about who smuggled the artifacts," Kate said. "It may not have been the old ladies at all."

Our plan was unraveling fast. I wasn't sure if Reese and Richard were able to see what was going on anymore, and Fern wouldn't be able to distract Grace and Derek for much longer. I saw Derek look down, spot me, and nudge his wife.

I grabbed the bag from the floor. "Come on. Let's get out of here."

"What?" Kate said, slipping off the barstool to follow me. "I thought the plan was to wait here and then Reese would swoop in."

I glanced back at the terrace as I darted across the landing toward the stairs. "I don't see Reese or Richard. If they can't see what's going on, that means we could be cornered by that bride and groom alone. We need to get out into the open. Buster and Mack are outside. Let's go find them."

I hurried down the stairs and out the revolving door of the hotel with Kate close behind me. I looked right and left. No sign of Buster or Mack, and they usually weren't known for blending in with the scenery. Where were they?

Kate gave me a little push from behind. "We have to keep moving. Derek and Grace are coming down the stairs after us."

I took off down the sidewalk, the Louis Vuitton duffel hooked over my shoulder. I heard Kate's high-heeled boots clopping behind me, and I made a mental note to personally buy her a pair of flats and make her wear them.

I paused at the crosswalk and Kate caught up to me. Glancing at the park across from us one way and the Grafton Street area to the other, I weighed which way to go until the walk signal flashed and the decision was made for me. We dashed toward the park, running along the sidewalk until we reached an entrance. I hoped Reese or Richard or Fern had seen us leave. I didn't have time to stop and call them.

"This is pretty," Kate said as we walked along a path shaded by tall trees.

I nodded as I headed further into St. Stephen's Green. I glanced behind me and didn't see anyone following us, so I slowed my pace.

"Now what do we do?" Kate asked.

"We need to circle back to the hotel," I said, as we came out into an open area with a small fountain. A slab of rock in the middle held a gunmetal gray stone statue of three cloaked people with water flowing out from under the slab.

"And hope Grace and Derek are gone?" Kate asked.

I peered around to the empty park benches and quiet pathway then walked behind the fountain that was bordered by a tall hedge. "We need to figure out how we could have been so wrong. I was positive one of the ladies from the genealogy tour was the smuggler and killer."

"Well, you were half right."

Kate and I both turned at the sound of the vaguely familiar Irish accent.

32

"Seamus?" I asked, recognizing the bus driver for the old ladies. "What are you doing here?"

Kate nodded her head toward the gun he was holding at us. "I think he may be more than just a bus driver, Annabelle."

I pulled the bag closer to me. "You?"

As I stared at the sandy-haired man, it all made sense. He'd been there when both Colleen and Nancy had been attacked, but we'd never considered him as a suspect. As the driver, he'd also overheard everything we'd said when we'd discussed the case on the bus, and he'd had access to all of our bags. It would have been easy for him to lift Kate's green scarf and take the luggage tag from Colleen's bag. And what better way to steal and smuggle things than to do it while driving a tour group around. Drivers--like many service providers--became invisible, which is probably why we'd never even considered him as a suspect.

"But you're Irish," Kate said, her eyes not leaving the gun. "Why would you steal your own history?"

"What good does a bunch of old metal stuff do me, eh?" he said. "But I can get a pretty penny if I sell it. More than I make driving Americans."

"Okay, I get the money part," I said. "But why kill Colleen?"

"That one was getting too nosy." He shifted from one foot to the other. "She opened the wrong bag and saw things. She even took a piece, and I think she was planning to show folks."

"That's what she was going to ask me about," I said, remembered Colleen saying she needed to talk to me when we got off the bus at Dromoland. That also explained the brooch in her carry-on bag. "She had suspicions about you, but you overheard her."

Kate put a hand to her throat. "Did you really strangle her?"

He shook his head. "Wasn't me. I thought a good talking to would do her."

I saw some movement out of the corner of my eye. "It was you, wasn't it?" I asked as Deb walked up behind the driver.

Seamus jumped. "I didn't see yeh there. You put the heart crossways in me."

"Her?" Kate waved a hand at the plump woman.

“It had to be one of the women who wasn’t loaded,” I said. “One who would have only been able to afford a fake Louis. Reese told me Myrna and Betty Belle both had rich husbands. You’re one of the ones who didn’t, right?”

"Give me the bag," Deb said, her tentative smile replaced by a steely glare.

Kate gasped. "You strangled your friend?"

"She wasn't my friend," Deb said. "I tried to get her to shut up, but she kept going on about seeing the valuables in the bag and recognizing them from a museum we'd visited. I knew she was going to ruin everything."

"So you killed her." I took a step back and my shoulders brushed against the hedge. "But what's your connection to Seamus? Did you meet on your first trip to Ireland?"

Seamus jerked his head in her direction. "She's me cousin. Found me the first time she came over with Myrna. Got me the job driving the bus for the next trip."

"So the genealogy searches are legitimate," Kate said. "That's good to know."

I took a step closer to Kate and further from Seamus and his gun. "Whose idea was it to start stealing antiquities? How does it work?" I cocked my head at Seamus. "You swipe them and she sells them back in the U.S.?"

"I want that bag," Deb said through gritted teeth. "Hand it over, and he won't shoot you."

I tightened my grip. The bag may have been stuffed with nothing but Fern's ample collection of tea towels, but I wanted to keep both of them talking. Once we relinquished our leverage, I wasn't sure what would happen. Plus, the longer they talked the greater the chance one of our friends would find us.

I glanced over Seamus's shoulder, hoping to see Reese running up. No luck. For all I knew, he was back at the hotel being swarmed by bridesmaids with no clue we'd run out the front door.

"It's just the two of you then?" I said. "None of the other ladies are involved? This wasn't all Myrna's idea?"

"Myrna?" Deb said. "Why would she need the money? Her rich husbands drop dead as fast as she can marry them."

"So this is about money for you too?" Kate asked. "I thought Fern said all you ladies were loaded."

Deb's eyes narrowed. "All the others are. I'm the only one who isn't a wealthy widow."

"So how did this all play out?" I asked. "How do you go from meeting a long-lost relative to starting a smuggling ring together?"

Deb took a step toward us, and Kate and I both shuffled to the side. "Seamus has always been on the wrong side of the law. He confessed to me that he'd done some time for robbery around the same time I was going in all these small museums and manor houses. We got to talking one night over some pints and came up with the plan."

"And it's been going fine and all until you showed up," Seamus said.

"You consider killing one woman and bashing another over the head 'going fine?'" Kate asked.

I steadied my gaze at Seamus. "You were the one who attacked Nancy, weren't you? It makes sense. Deb was with the other ladies having tea while you followed her down to the train car." I shook my head, partially disgusted with myself for not putting it together sooner. "You were the only one we didn't think about when gathering alibis."

His cheeks flushed. "I didn't kill her, did I?"

Deb swung her eyes to him. "No you didn't. And we don't know what she knows or who she plans to tell."

"I'm surprised you didn't try to do her in at the hospital," I said to Deb.

She gave a curt shake of her head. "I would have if Myrna hadn't been dogging my steps. Plus, there were people everywhere."

"That's comforting," Kate whispered to me. "Unlike now."

I peered around us. Kate was right. Our corner of St. Stephen's Green seemed deserted. The darkening clouds overhead didn't help, and I expected anyone left in the park would soon be taking shelter. Our only hope was that the rainstorm might give us a chance to distract Seamus and Deb and escape.

"Enough talk." Deb stamped her foot. "Hand me that bag or my cousin here is going to shoot you both."

I swallowed hard. Either he was going to shoot us after we handed over the bag or as soon as they realized the antiquities were no longer inside. I gave a final sweeping glance around me.

"Fine." I started to extend my arm with the bag, but at the last second I tossed it into the fountain and pulled Kate with me behind the three stone figures.

"Idiot girl," Deb screeched. "Shoot them!"

I heard a gunshot hit stone, and Kate and I both ducked down.

"He's actually shooting at us," Kate said.

I tried to stay behind the three large stone figures as I

watched Deb lean over into the fountain in an attempt to fish out the Louis Vuitton bag, and Seamus tried to get us in his sights again. "I noticed."

Thunder rumbled, shaking the ground, and I pulled Kate down onto the ground. Screams were followed by splashes as I looked up and saw Buster and Mack lumbering up and launching Seamus and Deb into the fountain headfirst.

"That wasn't thunder," I said, watching Buster retrieve the gun from the fountain and point it at Seamus. "It was the Mighty Morphin Flower Arrangers!"

It wasn't their official name, but was something they liked to call themselves. Buster and Mack grinned when they heard it. If ever there were superhero florists, my big-hearted friends were it.

Mack lifted the dripping wet designer bag from the water and leveled a finger at the drenched Deb as she rolled over in the fountain. "If I were you, I wouldn't move."

As fat raindrops began to splatter onto the pavement, I saw Richard and Reese running up with what looked like a group of uniformed guards behind them.

Reese didn't stop until he'd reached me, and he pulled me into a tight embrace then held me out at arm's length, looking me up and down. "Are you okay? We heard a gunshot."

"I'm fine," I said, even though my heart was racing. “Where have you been? Where did you get all the backup?"

“Mobbed by bridesmaids on the terrace,” Richard said with a shudder. “It was awful.”

Kate put a hand on one hip. “Worse than being shot at?”

“Did I mention there were also flower girls?” Richard said.

"Kate sent us a group text when you left the hotel," Reese explained. "Richard and I were looking for you when we saw a couple of guards on patrol."

I turned to Kate. "You texted while we were running?"

She shrugged. "I'm good at multitasking."

"But you didn't say where you were going," Richard said, his voice higher than usual. "We were going crazy looking for you."

"Well, one of us was closer to crazy than the other," Reese said so only I could hear him.

Richard's attention went to the figures in the fountain. "What's the bus driver doing here?"

"He's the thief and smuggler," I said. "Along with his cousin, Deb."

"The mousy one?" Richard looked like he couldn't believe what we were saying. "They're behind everything?"

"Deb killed Colleen and Seamus attacked Nancy," Kate said.

"But I didn't kill her," Seamus called out from where he sat in the fountain.

"You can't prove anything," Deb said as she and Seamus were hoisted out of the fountain by a pair of guards.

Kate pulled her phone out of her pocket. "Sure we can. I recorded everything." She grinned at the youngest looking guard. "Give me your digits, and I'll send you the file."

The rain continued to fall as the two were hauled away, and Reese pulled me close again. "I'm so relieved you're okay," he murmured into my ear.

"Me too." I shivered even though his arms were warm, and I suspected it might be the shock from being held at gunpoint.

"You're alive," Fern said as he ran up, his saffron kilt flapping open and flashing plenty of thigh. He leaned against Richard to catch his breath. "I got distracted by those newlyweds and then you were gone. I got Kate's text and then I heard a gunshot." He stifled a sob. "Who got shot?"

Richard tried to extricate himself from Fern. "No one."

"That's not exactly true," Mack said as he held up the soaking Louis Vuitton bag, which now sported a bullet hole in one side.

"Louis!" Fern screamed and swooned against Richard, who buckled under the weight.

"Maybe it can be repaired," Kate said. "I have an excellent leather repair man in Old Town."

"It's vintage," Fern sniffled.

Richard patted him brusquely on the back. "Maybe it's the universe telling you to treat yourself to a new bag."

Fern perked up. "I like the way you think, sweetie. I have had my eye on the new black checkerboard duffels from the spring collection."

"By the way," Reese said to Fern, "who were those people you were talking to in the hotel?"

"Grace and Derek?" Fern frowned. "Those newlyweds are on my list. I told them I was too busy to talk, but they wouldn't stop asking me questions."

"Those are the newlyweds who've been following you?" Reese asked. "That's interesting."

Kate held out her hands as the raindrops spilled through the canopy of leaves overhead. "Should we get back to the hotel before we're all soaked?"

"We'd better hurry," Richard said, waving at Buster and Mack. "If all that leather shrinks, it could cut off their circulation."

"No more casualties," I said, linking my hand with Reese's as we walked back through the park. "I'm ready for this to be a normal trip."

Reese let out a breath and squeezed my hand. "I don't think I've ever been on a normal trip with you."

"That makes two of us," Richard said.

"I promise the rest of our time in Ireland will be completely uneventful," I said. "All two days of it."

Richard gave me a side-eye glance. "When have I heard that before, darling?"

33

"I feel like a new person," I said, walking arm in arm with Reese down the stairs of The Shelbourne Hotel the next day. "It's amazing what a good night's sleep and not being worried about a criminal on the loose will do for you."

"I think we may have slept too well," Reese said, nuzzling my neck. "We missed breakfast. And lunch."

"That's fine by me," I said. "This hotel is famous for its afternoon tea anyway."

As we entered the foyer, I glanced over at The Lord Mayor's Lounge, bright and airy and filled with celadon-green and butter-yellow wingback chairs and curved high-backed settees. Tall windows looked out onto the sidewalk, and chandeliers dripping with crystals hung from various points throughout the room. I noticed that it was set for tea, and waiters moved from table to table pouring champagne and depositing silver tiered stands of tea sandwiches and confections. Flowery china cups clinked as they were set in saucers, and the air even held the scent of sugar.

"Who's Fern sitting with?" Reese asked, peering across the room to where Fern appeared to be holding court at a round table set in front of a fireplace and tall gilded mirror.

"That's the American genealogy tour group," I said. "What's left of them anyway."

I noticed that steely-haired Myrna looked a bit shell-shocked, not surprising since she'd recently discovered that her right-hand woman had been using the tours to smuggle Irish antiquities out of the country. I imagined that was enough to ruffle even the staunchest of feathers.

"At least Fern seems to be distracting them," Reese said.

At that moment Fern said something that made the entire table break out in a cacophony of tittering. I noticed a few women blush and could easily imagine the stories Fern was telling. He was notorious for telling off-color jokes to loosen up bridal parties and keep brides from getting stressed, so I knew the tales he was telling the old ladies were probably not suitable for work and certainly not suitable for high tea.

"Why don't I go check on him," I said, giving my boyfriend's hand a squeeze.

Reese looked out the front of the hotel. "Sounds good. I actually see a couple of people I need to talk to."

Before I could ask him who he knew in Dublin, he was out the revolving door. I made my way across the dining room to Fern's table.

"Annabelle," he said when he saw me. "The ladies and I were just having a spot of tea while I told them about some of our wildest weddings. Pull up a chair, sweetie."

"Reese and I are actually on our way out to do some sightseeing." I smiled at the ladies as Fern glanced at his watch. "But I wanted to come say goodbye in case I don't see you all before we leave tomorrow."

Betty Belle stood up and pulled me into a tight hug. "It sure was a pleasure to meet you, sugar. And the girls and I can't thank you enough for finding out who killed Colleen."

"And attacked Nancy," another said from the end of the table.

"I'm not the least bit surprised," Betty Belle whispered in my ear. "That Deb was wound too tight if you ask me. She was bound to snap sometime."

"I'm glad we got justice for Colleen," I said. "She seemed like a nice woman."

Betty Belle gave me a final squeeze before releasing me.

Myrna stood, her back stiff. "Yes, we owe you a debt of gratitude." She smiled at me as she held out a hand. "I understand this is something you do often."

I shot a look at Fern who was pointedly looking at the scone on his plate. "Not often, but I'm glad we were able to help. I hope you can enjoy the last few days of your trip."

"Luckily, we're here until we leave," Betty Belle said with a snort of laughter. "Especially since we lost our driver."

Myrna pressed her lips together. "I feel like a fool for being taken in by Seamus and Deb."

I patted her arm. "You shouldn't be too hard on yourself." I thought about the cold-blooded killers I'd thought were the sweetest people in the world. "It happens to the best of us."

"I'm just glad one of us didn't get impaled on an ice sculpture," one of the ladies said.

Another nodded and looked askance at the sweets on her plate. "Or get poisoned with a chocolate truffle."

I crossed my arms and stared at Fern. "You've been quite the storyteller, haven't you?"

His cheeks became a mottled patchwork of pink, but his eyes lit up as he glanced behind me. "Hello there, Detective."

I turned as Reese slipped his hand in mine and grinned at me. "Ready to go?"

I gave Fern what I hoped was a stern look as I waved goodbye to the ladies and we weaved our way back through the dining room to the foyer. "Did you talk to the people you needed to?"

"Actually, I did," he said as we baby stepped through the revolving door together. "You know the newlywed couple that's been following you around?"

I rolled my eyes. "Grace and Derek. Are they still here?"

"Not for long," Reese said once we'd spilled out onto the sidewalk. "I thought I recognized them when I saw Fern talking to them yesterday. I made a few calls and sent a phone pic of them to my buddies back at the station."

I felt my stomach drop. "Don't tell me they're criminals."

"Nope," he said. "Reporters. They work for *DC Life* magazine."

"Okay," I said. "What are they doing over here pretending to be on their honeymoon?"

"They've been researching a story about the wedding planning team with all the murders at their weddings. Between Fern giving them your itinerary and Kate posting online every time you arrived at a new venue, you weren't hard to track."

My stomach tightened into a hard knot. I knew Instagram would be our undoing. "Us? They're printing an article about all the murders that have taken place at Wedding Belles weddings?" I felt tears prick the backs of my eyes. "That will destroy my business. No one will hire us after they read that. Do they mention Richard and Fern and the guys from Lush too?"

"They were planning to," Reese said, turning and holding both of my arms. "But that was before I stopped them."

"You stopped them?" I heard my voice crack. "How?"

"I mentioned the various ways they'd probably impeded the investigations, as well as potential charges for concealing their identities to the Gardaí here." He winked. "I might have implied they would face charges both here and back in the U.S."

I threw my arms around his neck. "Have I told you how much I love you?"

"Not in the past hour," he said, chuckling.

I kissed him hard, not caring that we were standing on the sidewalk in front of the hotel as people walked around us. I pulled back and raised an eyebrow at him. "You still want to go sightseeing?"

"It seems a shame to come to Dublin and not see anything," he said.

A cherry-red double-decker bus pulled to a stop at the corner. "We aren't going on that are we?"

He laughed again. "No." He gestured to a black cab idling at the curb. "I hired us a classic black cab."

"Annabelle!" I heard the deep bellowing voice and looked up to see Buster and Mack waving wildly from the upper, open-air level of the double-decker bus.

I waved back as the bus lurched forward then said to Reese, "You don't think Richard and Kate are on there too, do you?"

He shrugged. "Maybe they slept in."

"That would make sense for Kate, but Richard doesn't sleep in."

Reese held the door to the cab open for me. "I'm sure we'll catch up to them later."

I got inside and settled myself on the leather seats, enjoying the roomy interior of the classic car. Reese sat next to me and draped his arm over my shoulders, then tapped the driver.

Our car wound through the streets of Dublin as the driver narrated what we were seeing, skirting us past Trinity College and Christ Church Cathedral then along the Liffey River. He slowed when we reached a white iron pedestrian bridge. "Here yeh are, lad."

"I thought we'd walk across the bridge," Reese said, hopping out of the cab and offering me his hand.

I followed him, breathing in the fresh cool air and looking up as we walked beneath one of the pointed metal arches spanning both sides of the bridge and topped with a streetlamp. Once we'd reached the middle of the bridge, Reese stopped. I looked down the river and could see most of Dublin spread out before me. "It's beautiful."

"It seemed like a perfect place." His voice shook slightly as he took both my hands.

I looked over and spotted two familiar figures at the other

end of the bridge. "Why are Richard and Kate here?" I squinted. "And why is Richard holding a bottle of something?"

"It's champagne." Reese said. "I have to come clean, babe. Richard wasn't only telling me things about the case and helping me arrange a flight over here. He was also helping me plan this."

"Plan what?" I looked back at him and saw that he was kneeling down on one knee in front of me.

My heart started pounding and my mouth went dry. I'd seen enough proposals in my life to know the signs. I'd even helped plan a few myself. I'd just never given much thought to being on the receiving end of one.

"What are you . . .?" The words died in my throat as he popped open a small jewelry box and a diamond ring sparkled up at me.

"Annabelle Archer," he said, his voice thick with emotion, "you are the most fascinating, frustrating woman I've ever known. Will you marry me?"

The world seemed to stand still as I glanced over at Richard with the bottle of champagne and Kate holding her phone out, clearly recording this moment. I looked down at the ring glittering in the box and then at Reese's hazel eyes, which had deepened to green. After living my life around matrimony for so long, it felt almost surreal that I could be a bride.

"I already got Richard's blessing," Reese said, his face earnest.

I felt tears filling my eyes. "You did?"

"Are you kidding?" Reese said. "I was afraid if I didn't, he'd bake me a batch of Ex-Lax brownies."

"In that case," I said, touching his cheek. "Yes. Of course I'll marry you."

Beaming, he slid the ring onto my finger, and stood up, sweeping me off my feet and into a deep kiss. I could hear whooping and cheering behind us, and I recognized Kate's catcall. All my nerves and anxiety seemed to evaporate as we kissed, his strong arms holding me tight.

When he pulled away, I gazed up at him. "You know you're stuck with them now." I motioned my head to where Kate was still cheering and Richard was tapping his foot impatiently. I noticed a cab screech to a stop and Fern, Buster, and Mack all piled out and started waving and clapping.

"It's a package deal. I always knew that." He kissed me again, this time softly. "And to be honest, they feel like they're my friends too at this point."

"You know they love you," I said.

"They love me because I love you," he said.

I held out my finger to admire my new ring. "Same thing."

"Yeah," he grinned at me and swung me around in a circle. "I guess it is."

Did you enjoy this book? You can make a big difference!

I'm extremely lucky to have a loyal bunch of readers, and honest reviews are the best way to help bring my books to the attention of new readers.

If you enjoyed *Irish Aisles Are Smiling*, I would be forever grateful if you could spend two minutes leaving a review (it can be as short as you like) on Goodreads, Bookbub, or your favorite retailer.

Thanks for reading and reviewing!

ALSO BY LAURA DURHAM

Read the entire Annabelle Archer Series in order:

Better Off Wed

For Better Or Hearse

Dead Ringer

Review To A Kill

Death On The Aisle

Night of the Living Wed

Eat, Prey, Love

Groomed For Murder

Wed or Alive

To Love and To Perish

Marry & Bright

The Truffle with Weddings

Irish Aisles are Smiling

To get notices whenever I release a new book, follow me on BookBub:

https://www.bookbub.com/profile/laura-durham

FREE DOWNLOAD!

A GLAMOROUS BRIDAL SHOW.
A CLEVER JEWELRY HEIST.

CAN ANNABELLE TRACK DOWN THE BAUBLES AND NAB A BURGLAR?

amazon kindle

nook

kobo

iBooks

Get your free copy of the novella "Dead Ringer" when you sign up to the author's mailing list.

Get started here:

deadringer.lauradurham.com

ACKNOWLEDGMENTS

This book was inspired by a month we spent driving around Ireland last year. Like Annabelle and crew, we lost a sideview mirror and a little bit of our sanity driving on the narrow roads. We fell in love with the beautiful country, the warm people, and the fabulous castles! I couldn't include every spot we visited, but I included a few.

As always, an enormous thank you to all of my wonderful readers, especially my beta readers and my review team. I never give you enough time, but you always come through for me. A special shout-out to the beta readers who caught all my goofs this time: Patricia Joyner, Carol Spayde, Karen Diamond, Sheila Kraemer, Elizabeth Brown, and Sandra Anderson, Tony Noice, and Cathy Jaquette. Thank you!!

A warm thank you to my wonderful copyeditor Sandy Chance. One day I'll get all those hyphens right!

A heartfelt thank you to everyone who leaves reviews. They really make a difference, and I am grateful for every one of them!

As always, all my love to my husband and kids. I wouldn't want to trek all over Ireland (and the world) with anyone else!

ABOUT THE AUTHOR

Laura Durham has been writing for as long as she can remember and has been plotting murders since she began planning weddings over twenty years ago in Washington, DC. Her first novel, BETTER OFF WED, won the Agatha Award for Best First Novel.

When she isn't writing or wrangling brides, Laura loves traveling with her family, standup paddling, perfecting the perfect brownie recipe, and reading obsessively.

She loves hearing from readers and she would love to hear from you! Send an email or connect on Facebook, Instagram, or Twitter (click the icons below).

Find me on:
www.lauradurham.com
laura@lauradurham.com

facebook.com/authorlauradurham
twitter.com/reallauradurham
instagram.com/lauradurhamauthor

CPSIA information can be obtained
at www.ICGtesting.com
Printed in the USA
LVHW091829120120
643360LV00003B/343/P

9 781949 496215